BOOKS BY BILL MYERS

Children's Series
McGee and Me! (12 books)

The Incredible Worlds of Wally McDoogle:
—*My Life As a Smashed Burrito with Extra Hot Sauce*
—*My Life As Alien Monster Bait*
—*My Life As a Broken Bungee Cord*
—*My Life As Crocodile Junk Food*
—*My Life As Dinosaur Dental Floss*
—*My Life As a Torpedo Test Target*
—*My Life As a Human Hockey Puck*
—*My Life As an Afterthought Astronaut*
—*My Life As Reindeer Road Kill*
—*My Life As a Toasted Time Traveler*
—*My Life As Polluted Pond Scum*

Fantasy Series
Journeys to Fayrah:
—*The Portal*
—*The Experiment*
—*The Whirlwind*
—*The Tablet*

Teen Series
Forbidden Doors:
—*The Society*
—*The Deceived*
—*The Spell*
—*The Haunting*
—*The Guardian*
—*The Encounter*

Adult Books
Christ B.C.
Blood of Heaven

the incredible worlds of **Wally McDoogle**

MY LiFe as alien Monster bait

BILL MYERS

WORD PUBLISHING
Dallas·London·Vancouver·Melbourne

MY LIFE AS ALIEN MONSTER BAIT

Unless otherwise indicated, Scripture quotations are from the *International Children's Bible, New Century Version*, copyright © 1983, 1986, 1988 by Word Publishing.

Scripture quotations marked (NIV) are from The New International Version of the Bible, copyright © 1978 by the New York International Bible Society.

Library of Congress Cataloging-in-Publication Data

Myers, Bill, 1953–
    My life as alien monster bait / Bill Myers
        p. cm. — (The incredible worlds of Wally McDoogle ; #2)

    Summary: Wally's pride gets out of control when he is chosen by a movie company to be in the film they are making in Middletown, until he discovers the cost of true friendship and God's desire for humility.
    ISBN 0–8499–3403–6
    [1. Motion pictures—Production and direction—Fiction. 2. Christian life—Fiction. 3. Humorous stories.] I. Title. II. Series: Myers, Bill, 1953– Incredible worlds of Wally McDoogle ; #2
PZ7.M98234Myp 1993
[Fic]—dc20   92–45184
                                      CIP
                                        AC

Printed in the United States of America

99 00 QBP 22

To Bob and Ilene—
For your love and support these many years.

Never think that some people are more important than others.

—James 2:1

Contents

Chapter 1

Just for Starters . . .

Science class was created for sleep.

That's pretty obvious.

The way I figure it, God knew kids would like to stay up late. He also knew they'd hate English, geography, math, and all the other brain bruisers grownups would dream up. So He created something like science class (which we can't possibly understand anyway) so we can catch some zzz's and keep staying up late.

Simple, right?

Not to Reptile Man. That's what we call Mr. Reptenson, our science teacher. He seems to think the life stages of a moth are more important than what late-night talk shows have to say.

Talk about a weird set of values.

At the moment Reptile Man was droning on about carbon dioxide, oxygen, and photo-something-or-other. You know, the usual non-stop, action/adventure, science stuff.

I slipped my leg under my seat and sat on it. Then I threw a look over to Opera. He was my best friend for as long as I can remember. Well, ever since last summer at Camp Whacko. That's because he's a fellow Dork-oid. You know, *"Dork-oids"* . . .

—the ones wearing the same haircuts everyone else wore five years ago.

—the ones wearing their brother or sister's hand-me-downs that are still just a little too big.

—the ones always picked last when choosing sides for any sports of any kind.

Or, as the dictionary reads:

Dork-oids (dor·koids´) n. 1. Bottom of the human food chain. 2. Triple A losers.

Anyway, we Dork-oids always stick together. Through thick or thin, we're always there for each other. In fact, we even have our own hand signal—a clinched fist with the little finger raised. It means, "I know it's not easy being the All-School Fool, but hang in there 'cause you've got company."

Opera was already nodding off. I tell you, the guy could sleep through anything—except classical music. And, of course, breakfast . . . or lunch . . . or dinner . . . or the sound of any potato chip bag being opened within a mile.

Reptile Man stood behind the counter at the front of the room. I was way in the back. No way could he see me. So I closed my eyes for just a second, or two, or twenty, or—

"Mr. McDoogle?"

I jerked and blinked awake.

"Would you be so kind as to come up and demonstrate?"

I swallowed nervously. I had no idea what the guy was talking about, so I tried to stall. "I uh . . . I don't think I'm qualified."

Everyone giggled.

"Mr. McDoogle, if you're a human being who inhales oxygen and exhales carbon dioxide, believe me, you qualify."

More giggles.

One other thing I forgot to mention about Reptile Man—he hated me. The guy always picked on me. The best I figure, he knew I was the only one in the school who couldn't beat him up. And since he had to take out his frustrations on somebody, and since I was the only one available . . . well, there I was . . . ready, willing, and not so able.

"Mr. McDoogle . . . we're waiting . . . "

"Oh . . . right," I stuttered. "No problem." I stood up, took one step forward, then fell flat on my face. Seems my eyes weren't the only things that had fallen asleep. My leg had also taken a little nap. Of course everyone laughed. And of course I jumped up, giving my usual McDoogle-the-idiot grin. It's like one of my trademarks. McDonald's has its golden arches; I've got my idiot grin.

I half limped, half staggered to the front of the class. (My foot was a slow riser.)

A glass beaker sat on the counter. There was some liquid inside it and a glass tube, like a straw.

Reptile Man was wet with perspiration. He was always wet with perspiration. You could put him in the middle of Antarctica and there'd still be sweat on his forehead. Of course, it would be in the form of giant icicles, but you probably get the picture.

He picked up the beaker of liquid. "Go ahead," he grinned as he handed it to me.

It was a setup, I could tell.

The class waited in eager anticipation.

I looked to Opera, hoping for a clue. But he was still off in la-la-land. By the smile on his lips, he was either dreaming about Mozart, or falling into a giant vat of Hostess Twinkie filling.

I took the beaker.

The class chuckled.

"Go ahead," Reptile Man said, motioning to the straw.

I put my mouth to it.

They giggled louder.

Now I figured I had two choices . . . suck in or blow out. If I sucked in, the liquid would probably poison me, and Reptile Man would have accomplished his lifelong goal.

On the other hand, if it were a liquid explosive and I blew out, I'd probably level the entire room . . . which would probably mean after-school detention for at least thirty to forty years.

Decisions, decisions . . .

I took one last look at my classmates. Most of them were bullys or wiseacres. I know God wants us to love everybody, but I figured the world would probably be a safer and better place without them. So . . . I took a deep breath and was about to blow us all to kingdom come when suddenly I saw her . . . Melissa Sue Avarice—the most beautiful girl in Olympic Heights Middle School.

All of my life I'd tried to get her to notice me. And all of my life, she rated me right up there with your basic slug slime. But now . . . now she was actually smiling at me. Me! Wally McDoogle! Wally McDoogle, All-American Oddball! Well, maybe she wasn't exactly smiling at me. . . . Maybe it was more like laughing. But the point is

we made contact. Melissa Sue and me. And it
was...
M A G I C.
Well, I knew what had to be done. I had to save
Missy (that's what we, her closest friends, call
her). No doubt about it, I had to save Missy's life.
Regardless of the dangers to my own person, I had
to do what I had to do. I wrapped my mouth
around the straw and began to draw the deadly
liquid toward my mouth when suddenly—

"Attention, please... attention..."

It was the PA speaker. There was a loud squeal
of feedback. That meant it was Vice Principal
Watkins. The guy never could get the hang of using
the intercom.

*"Attention please... SQUEAL... A motion-
picture company has come to town. Sludge Productions will hold auditions for their next movie,
'Mutant from Mars,'... SQUEAL... this afternoon, on the stage in the auditorium. All those
interested in trying... S Q U E A L...Ahem...
all those interested in trying out for a part, please
meet at the hallway stage door at 3:30 this afternoon. Thank you."*

That was it. My entire life had changed in that short announcement. Forget this dorky beaker in my hand, forget sacrificing my life, forget Missy . . . (Well, let's not be hasty. We'll remember Missy awhile longer if you don't mind.) The point is I was going to be a star. I knew it.

The only problem was that every other kid in the school knew he or she was going to be a star, too. Suddenly our classroom was buzzing. Every classroom was buzzing. Everyone was going to audition.

The bell rang, and we all headed for the door. Reptile Man was wiping his forehead and shouting something about, "Remember the Science Fair, everyone must participate." But no one heard. Everyone was too excited about the audition, about being in the movies.

Everyone but Reptile Man. He was still shouting. He probably figured he wouldn't have a chance to be a movie star. Then again, maybe they needed someone to play the Martian Mutant. . . .

* * * * *

"So what do you think?" Opera shouted.

"About the auditions?" I yelled.

We were playing Dodge Ball in the gym. You

know, the game where you hit the guys on the other team with the ball and put 'em out.

"I'm not talking about the auditions," Opera hollered. "I'm talking about the Science Fair—the one Reptile Man says we have to enter. You wanna be partners?"

WHOOSH! A ball sailed past, missing my head by an inch. Rats! If I had been paying attention, I could have gotten it to hit me. That's what those of us in the lack-of-muscles department try to do. We try to get out of the game as soon as possible, so there's less time to make fools of ourselves.

"Since when did he say anything about the Science Fair?" I shouted.

WHOOSH! Rats! Missed me again.

"Must of been when you were sleeping."

"Me sleeping!" I shouted. "What about you?"

WHOOSH! WHOOSH! Amazing. Two balls at a time and they still can't hit me. The jocks must be having an off day.

"You were the one snoozing away," I shouted, "how could you hear him?"

"I just rest half my brain at a time."

"You what?"

WHOOSH! Still no luck.

"So do you or don't you want to be partners?" he shouted.

"Sure," I yelled, doing my best to jump in front of a ball but missing it by a mile. "What's our subject?"

"Fleas," Opera shouted back.

"FLEAS?" I yelled. "What half of your brain's awake, now?"

"The reproductive cycle of fleas!" he hollered.

WHOOSH!

"Why would you want to do a science project—

WHOOSH! WHOOSH!

—on fleas?" I shouted.

"Why not?" he yelled.

He had me there. How could anyone argue with that type of logic?

"Hey, look!" he shouted. "We're the only ones left."

I glanced around. It was true. Everyone else on our team had been hit. They were all cheering us on from the sidelines. They were all shouting for us to catch a ball so they could come back in. They were all expecting us to be heroes.

"I hate it when this happens," I sighed.

"Me, too," Opera agreed. "Look out, here they come!"

I turned around just in time to see the other team fire all five balls at us at once . . .

WHOOSH! WHOOSH! WHOOSH! WHOOSH!
K-THWACK!!

The K-THWACK was the ball nailing my noggin. Suddenly I heard bells. Suddenly I had a hard time finding my legs. "Fleas," I mumbled just before hitting the floor. "Sure, why not . . ."

*   *   *   *   *

The line for the audition stretched from the stage door, around the hall, down the stairs, and into the cafeteria. (Like I said, everyone wanted to be a star.) Luckily, it moved pretty fast. Unfortunately, I was about to find out why.

At last I rounded the final corner. The door was just ahead. Only a handful of kids separated me from my destiny.

I spotted Wall Street. She was my other best friend from camp. Another Dork-oid. She had just come back from the grocery store where she had bought a bunch of pop. Now she moved down the line selling it at a buck a can. (Hey, we don't call her Wall Street for nothing.) Of course, everybody complained, but lots of kids were buying, too.

"Wally," she called. "I thought you were going to write for the movies, not star in them."

"I know," I shrugged, "but sometimes you gotta start at the bottom."

"Yeah, I suppose. Hey, you want some pop?"

"Sure, how much?"

"Well, since you're a friend, let's make it a buck fifty and call it even."

Good ol' Wall Street. She planned to make her first million before she turned fifteen.

Suddenly there was a loud scream. It came from behind the stage door.

"What's that?" I stiffened.

"They do that every once in a while," Wall Street shrugged. "No biggie."

But a couple kids behind me thought it was a "biggie." They quickly packed up and headed home. So did three or four in front of me. Hmmm. Maybe they knew something I didn't.

The door creaked open. It was dark inside—very dark. The kid in the front of the line hesitated.

"Next!" a voice cried from somewhere deep in the blackness.

The kid took a deep breath.

"Next!" the voice commanded.

Finally the kid stepped through the door. The darkness seemed to swallow him up as the door slammed with a foreboding boom.

A couple more folks packed up and left.

"Well, good luck!" Wall Street called as she headed down the line.

"Yeah," I said, trying to find my voice, "thanks a lot."

After a moment the door opened again. The next kid stepped inside to meet his fate. A minute later there was another terrifying scream, scarier than the last.

Four more kids suddenly thought it was a good idea to split.

My heart started pounding faster. It's not that I was scared. It's just— Well, all right, I was scared. A lot scared. What was going on in there, anyway?

Now, there was just one girl between me and the door. The door which once again slowly creaked open.

"Next," the voice called from inside the darkness.

The girl turned to me, "You want to go?" she offered.

"Thanks," I said, "but I don't believe in cuts. It's not fair to the others. You go ahead."

"Oh." She sounded a little disappointed.

"Next," the voice demanded from inside the darkness.

"Well, here goes." She tried to look happy. But there was something about her pale face, her dripping forehead, and shaking hands that said she wasn't exactly thrilled with the idea. Finally, with a deep breath, she stepped into the blackness.

Too bad, I thought as the door slammed shut. *She seemed like such a nice kid.*

I waited. There was no scream. No nothing. Suddenly I wondered, *Why do kids only go in this door and never come out?* Other questions started, like, *What photo would my folks choose to put on the milk cartons?*

Before I had any answers, the door creaked open. "Next," the voice called.

I tried to swallow, but there wasn't anything to swallow. My mouth was as dry as cotton. Make that freeze-dried cotton. Make that freeze-dried cotton in the middle of the Sahara Desert.

"Next!" the voice ordered.

I took a deep breath and said a little prayer. *"Please God, I'm sorry about wanting to blow up the science class."* It may seem weird, but I figured if I'm going to die and meet God, the fewer things I had to apologize for, the better . . .

I stepped inside the black room. The door closed behind me with a loud boom . . .

Chapter 2

Behind the Closed Door . . .

It took a second for my eyes to get used to the
dark. Suddenly, I noticed a skinny guy standing
beside me. He wore a silk shirt unbuttoned half
way down his chest, sunglasses shoved atop his
head. In his hand was a clipboard. He peered
down at me over the top of it.

"Well now," he grinned. "You just might do . . .
You just might do nicely."

He started forward. "This way, please."

I followed.

At the far end of the stage, a woman and a tired
old man sat behind a table. They were going
through a bunch of papers and photos and stuff.
When we arrived, Mr. Hollywood motioned for me
to the empty chair in front of them.

"Sit here," he ordered.

I obeyed.

The woman looked up. She was instant smiles and friendliness. "Well, now Mr. . . . Mr. . . . "

"Uh, Wally," I said.

"Well, now, Mr. Wally, what exactly—"

"No," I corrected, "McDoogle."

"What?"

"McDoogle," I repeated.

"I'm sorry, what's—"

"I'm a McDoogle."

"What's a McDoogle?"

"Me."

"You?"

"That's my name."

"But you just said your name was—"

"It is."

"Then how can it be—" Her smile was drooping slightly.

"Wally McDoogle!" I blurted out just a little too loudly. "My name is Wally McDoogle."

All the shouting caused the tired, old man to look up. I smiled weakly. Things were not going as I planned. It was time to turn on the famous McDoogle charm. "I've seen all your movies." *Liar,* I thought. *You don't know them from Adam. Or Eve. But I hoped God would cut me a little slack.*

I hoped wrong.

"Actually," the older man scowled, "we're only

the casting directors. You haven't seen a thing
we've done."

"Oh, right, yeah." *So much for slack.*

"Well, Mr. . . . McDoogle," the woman turned up
her fakey smile to HIGH. "Have you had any acting experience?"

"Absolutely!" Again I was just a little too loud.

"Really . . . " the older man suddenly sounded
less tired. "And what was your latest role?"

"A donkey!" I was shouting again. I tried to talk
softer. Unfortunately, it came out more like a des-
perate whisper. "In the Christmas pageant. Well,
not the whole donkey. Just the back half. Jason
Hampsten played the head. I played the back. Of
course, Jason got to do all the talking, we were a
talking donkey, but I had to follow him all around
and stay in step, otherwise we would trip up and—"

The older man cut me off. "Mr. Wally . . . "

"McDoogle," the woman corrected.

"What?" he asked

"McDoogle," she repeated.

"What's a *McDoog—*?"

"Wally, will be fine," I jumped in.

The woman's smile drooped again.

The man continued. "Mr. Wally, would you
scream for us?"

"Pardon me?"

"Scream."

"You mean . . . just . . . scream."

"Scream," he repeated.

"Don't you want me to read any lines or anything? I do a great Porky Pig imitation or maybe a—"

He gave a heavy sigh. "You're auditioning for the part of a child who is eaten by a Martian alien. All you need to do is scream."

"Well, okay. Just . . . scream," I repeated.

He nodded.

I took a deep breath.

He folded his arms and waited.

Well, it was now or never. My entire future hung in the balance. It was all up to my scream. I leaned back and gave it everything I had . . .

"AUHHHHHHHHHH!"

"Thank you, Mr. Wally, that was very—"

But I'd barely warmed up. I knew I could do better, so I tried again . . .

"AUHHHHHHHHHHHHHHHHHHHHHHHHHH!"

"Thank you, Mr. Wally—

And again . . .

"AUHHHHHHHHHHHHHHHHHHHHHHHHHHHHH HHHHHHHHH!"

"Mr. Wally, that will—

I was finally getting into it . . .

"AUHHHHHHHHHHHHHHHHHHHHHHHHHHHHH HHHHHHHHHHHHHHHHHHHHHHHHHHHHH!"

At last I was finished. I had to be. I'd run out of air. In fact, I was about to pass out.

Suddenly there was a bright flash. I looked around. It was Mr. Hollywood. He'd just taken a picture of me.

The tired old man looked back to his papers. It was like I had never been there. "Thank you, Mr. Wally."

"McDoogle," the woman corrected. "His name is—"

"Whatever," the man sighed. "Bring in the next one."

Hollywood helped me stand. I was still a little wobbly as he led me toward the opposite door.

It was gone. My big chance to break into pictures. I'd blown it!

"I can really do better," I called back to the table. "Honest, I can—"

Hollywood's grip tightened. "Let's go."

"If you'd just give me another—"

"That will be all, Mr. Wally," the older man sighed.

"McDoogle," the woman corrected.

"Whatever. Next!"

*   *   *   *   *

That night we all sat around the dinner table.

Mom; Dad; my little sister, Carrie; and Burt and
Brock my older, super-jock, twin brothers.

Mom tried her best to get a conversation going.
But she didn't have much luck.

"How was school today, Carrie?"

"Fine."

"How was football practice, Burt?"

"Fine.

"How is that new girl friend of yours, Brock?"

"Fine."

"Herb, how was your day at—"

"Fine," Dad interrupted, saving her the breath.

Mom looked back down to the food on her plate.
She gave a heavy sigh. So much for "quality time."

After dessert and a few more of my own "fines"
thrown in, I went up to my room. All the afternoon's
excitement started me thinking of another great
movie script. I grabbed ol' Betsy, my laptop computer, and flipped her on.

Soon, my fingers began flying across the keys. . . .

As we join Secret Agent James Brawn,
he is madly switching switches, dialing
dials and flipping er...flips.

Middletown's Nuclear Reactor is having a meltdown. The entire nation is in
danger. And, since it's James's day off,
he figured he'd swing by and brighten

up things a little by saving their day.

"Oh, no!" the helpless victims scream.
"We're all going to die. We're all going to glow like night lights!"

"Nonsense," James chuckles. "Just hand
me that stick of Juicy Fruit there, will
you, Herb?"

"But Wally," the man cries, "you're no
secret agent, you're my son, you're—"

"Father, it's time you know the truth.
By day I may be the incredibly nerdy
Wally McDoogle, but by night I'm (Ta-
da-daaaa!—that's secret agent music):
Brawn...James Brawn."

"I had no idea," Herb gasps.

"Yes, well, perhaps you'll think again
before asking me to clean out the cat
box. Now be a good fellow and hand me
that chewing gum."

Herb obeys. Immediately James rips off
the foil and stuffs it into an opening
labeled "Nuclear Fuse Box."

Instantly the reactor winds down. The
day is saved. The crowd goes wild. Someone begins shouting "BRAWN FOR PRESI-
DENT! BRAWN FOR PRESIDENT!" But James
has little time for their undying grati-
tude and praise...

His socks are ringing. That's right.
Secret agents always have fancy gizmos
and gadgets to help them save the world.
And James is no different.

Dashing into the nearest Men's Room,
he pulls up his pants and answers his
socks. "Brawn, here."

"Oh, James, we desperately need your
help." It's the President of Hollyweird.
Ever since they were forced to secede
from the Union (they were never really a
part of this country anyway) Hollyweird
has had problems.

"What's wrong, this time?" James sighs
his best secret agent sigh.

"Our commercials. Someone's stealing
our commercials."

"I don't under —"

"All those lovely advertisements
shouting at you to 'Buy, buy, buy...'
they're all disappearing, disappearing,
disappearing."

Quickly James reaches for his wallet
and unfolds it into a giant screen TV.
(A little invention allowing him to
catch all his favorite day-time soaps.)

"Great Granola, Mr. President!" James
shouts. "You're right. There are no

commercials anywhere. But how can—"

Suddenly another voice vibrates through our hero's socks.

"I'm holding them ranssssssom, Mr. Brawn."

Before you can say "How much weirder is this story going to get," James recognizes the voice. "Lizard Lips?" he shouts, "Is that you?"

"That isssss correct," the voice hisses.

Once a famous monster starring in several old Japanese Sci-Fi movies, Lizard Lips' popularity had slipped over the years. Now, this three-hundred-foot-long lizard was doing everything she could to get back on top.

She continued talking. "Hollyweird mussssst get me into three Sssstar Trek episssssodesss and pay me five gazillion dollarssss by midnight. Otherwisssse, there'll never be another commercial again."

"But . . . "

"Sssssee you in the moviessssss." There was a loud click. Lizard Lips hung up.

"Mr. President," James shouts, "did you hear that?"

"What will we do?" the President cries. "What will we do?"

"Relax, Sir. I'll take care of this personally."

"Oh, thank you, James, thank you."

With that, James pulls down his pant legs, steps out of the Men's Room, and gives three low whistles. Immediately his remote controlled Lear jet roars to his side. Racing up the plane's steps, James waves a fond farewell to the citizens of Middletown, before climbing behind the wheel, shifting into first, and laying a patch of rubber as he roars off to Hollyweird.

There were only 28.3 minutes to stop Lizard Lips before—

"Wally . . ."

I looked up from my computer. Mom was calling me.

"Can you come downstairs a moment?"

Rats, I hate getting interrupted when the story's cooking. "Okay!" I shouted. "Let me finish writing this one little—"

"You can finish it later. We need to talk."

"But, Mom."

"It'll only take a few minutes, Wally."

"Mom . . ." I planned to keep whining—you know, the ol' Wear-Her-Down game.

Then I heard the other voice. The voice of Dad. "*Now*, Son."

Well, so much for wearing her down. When Dad stepped in, the game always ended. If it didn't, he'd invent whole different games with titles like "You're Grounded for the Weekend" or "No TV for a month"—none of which are my favorites.

Mom continued, "Someone from Sludge Productions called. They want you to be in some sort of movie."

I don't remember turning Betsy off. I don't remember running downstairs to get the details. I don't even remember sleeping that night. But I do remember worrying what Sly Stallone, Arnie Schwarzenegger, and all those other superstars were going to do for a living now that the great Wally McDoogle had been discovered.

Chapter 3

School Daze

The following morning I was on automatic pilot. I'm sure I ate beakfast. (But I don't remember.) I'm sure I got dressed. (But I don't remember.) And I'm sure I walked out to the bus stop. I had to. How else did I get soaked when it splashed to a stop in front of me?

Besides dreaming how I was going to spend all my millions, I had spent most of that morning thinking how I'd break the news at school. I wouldn't do it immediately. No sir. I'd wait till the money rolled in. Then I'd have my private chauffeur start dropping me off. Better yet, I'd wait until Academy Awards night and thank all the little people that helped make it possible. Or—

But there was no "Or—" Because the moment the bus doors hissed open, I knew something was up. Most days you're lucky to get a grunt out of Mr. Kauffman, our bus driver. Or, when he's feeling particularly frisky, maybe a "I told you kids to be quiet!"

Not today. Today as I stumbled up the steps he greeted me with a "Good morning, Wally."

I stopped a moment, startled. He tried to smile, but it came off more like a snarl. Still, I appreciated the effort.

Next, I noticed the kids. They were all staring at me. But it wasn't the usual stare. You know, the glare stare that says, "Don't you even think of sitting beside me."

This was a different type of stare. I couldn't figure it out.

Suddenly the bus lurched into gear. I did my usual stagger and tumble routine toward the back until I spotted an empty seat and crashed into it.

When I looked up, I saw everyone was STILL staring at me. I went through the standard idiot checklist.

> Nose clean? .... *Check.*
> Shirt clean? .... *Check.*
> Pants zipped up? .... *Check.*

So why was everyone staring?

"Excuse me?" It was a second grader. Nice enough kid. It was the dreamy look she had in her eye that kind of threw me. She held out a piece of paper and a violet-blue crayon. "Can I have your autograph?"

Suddenly I understood. Mom must of called Aunt Thelma about my part in the movie. If you tell Aunt Thelma anything, it's kinda like taking out an ad in the paper . . . a big ad . . . on the front page. You see, Aunt Thelma loved to gossip. And telling her that her little nephew, Wally McDoogle, was going to be a movie star would be enough to keep her on the phone all day . . . and night . . . for months.

So that's what was going on. They already knew. It didn't matter that it wasn't official, that the director still had to make the final decision. And it didn't matter that I only had one line. . . . Actually it wasn't even a line, just a scream. The point is everybody thought I was a somebody.

And maybe, just maybe they had a point. Maybe I finally was a somebody.

But even as I took the pencil and piece of paper, even as I started writing, "See ya in the movies, kid," a still small voice whispered in the back of my head.

"Be careful . . . watch your attitude."

There's one thing nice about still, small voices in the back of your head—you can ignore them. You can drown them out . . . at least for a while.

*　　*　　*　　*　　*

"Hey, Wally, take a look at this."

It was Opera. As we headed down the hall, he kept shoving a little match box at me. So far it had been a pretty good day. Word of my fame spread like wildfire. My popularity rose at least 100 points before lunch. Already I'd had:

—Four autograph requests (mostly from the Crayola Crowd),

—Five "Hey Wallys" from the Jocks and Studs,

—Two "Wally my mans," from the Metal Heads,

—And almost a dozen smiles from the female types! That's right! A dozen! As in twelve! As in . . . well, you probably get the picture.

Suddenly it looked like my days as a Dork-oid were over. Imagine, just one little audition, one little phone call and suddenly I was king of the mountain. Well, maybe not king. Maybe prince. Well, maybe not prince but. . . . Well, at least I wasn't the court jester anymore.

So you can understand why I wasn't thrilled about Opera leeching on to me. Oh, sure, we were still friends and all. But . . . I don't know. It's like people were finally treating me like a somebody.

Me, Wally McDoogle. Then along comes this . . . this nobody (just like I used to be fourteen hours earlier). And his very presence reminds everyone of my past.

I felt pretty lousy thinking this. After all, we were best friends. But still . . .

"Hey, Wally." I looked up. It was Wall Street.

Oh, great, I thought, *another Dork-oid.*

"I heard the news," she grinned. "Congrats."

"Thanks," I said glancing around nervously. To be seen with one Dork-oid was bad enough. To be seen with two at the same time might be more than even my new reputation could handle.

"I just called up my stockbroker," she said as she patted the cellular phone inside her back pack. "I'm buying five shares of Sludge Productions."

"You don't have to—"

"Hey," she said, as she turned and headed off to class, "if you're going to be a star, the least I can do is make a buck off you!"

I grinned, grateful that she wasn't sticking around (and also feeling guilty at feeling grateful). What was wrong with me? We were friends, right? Then why was I embarrassed by her company?

Meanwhile Opera kept shoving his little match box at me. "Take a look inside," he nagged. "Take a look inside."

"What is it?" I finally snapped.

"Just look."

With a heavy sigh, I opened the box and looked inside. There were half a dozen little bugs. "What on earth is—"

"Fleas," he beamed.

"Fleas?" I shouted as I fumbled with the box, trying to close it. I only succeeded in dropping it to the floor. I guess instant fame is not a cure for terminal klutziness.

"It's for science class," Opera said, scooping up the box and counting the fleas inside. "Good, they're all here. I picked them off of Fluffy last night."

"What?"

"It's for our science project, don't you remember? We're going to be partners."

I remembered agreeing to something. But that was before the auditions. That was before last night's phone call. Before I became—

Suddenly I saw one of Melissa Sue's friends approach. You remember Melissa? *Missy*? From science class? Anyway, I stepped aside to let her friend pass, but she didn't pass. She came right at me!

Oh no, I thought, *what have I screwed up this time?*

But instead of firing off some classy put down, she smiled.

SHE SMILED!

I couldn't believe my luck! SHE SMILED. Oh, I guess I already said that. But at ME, she SMILED at ME! Of course, she wasn't Melissa Sue Avarice, but, hey, beggars can't be choosers.

Opera stared in disbelief.

"Hi," I finally managed to croak out.

Melissa's friend didn't answer. She just handed me a note.

"Thank you," I sort of mumbled as I took it.

She smiled again. Then she turned and sauntered down the hall as only rich and beautiful girls can saunter.

I stood watching—my mouth hanging down to my knees.

"Open it," Opera demanded.

I didn't hear. I was too dazed.

"Wally!"

"Huh?" I sounded about as intelligent as a steamed clam.

"Open it."

"Oh . . . yeah . . . sure . . ." I finally regained consciousness and struggled to unfold the note. Opera was immediately over my shoulder reading it. All it said was:

Can we get together?

Missy

I'm sure the rest of the day followed somehow . . . but I don't remember. I don't remember any of it . . . until that night. That's when we met the movie director . . . and Gertrude, his pet alien.

*   *   *   *   *

All I heard was the crunch of gravel as our car rolled down the road toward the deserted warehouse. This was it. In just a few minutes I would meet the director. In just a few minutes I would know if I really had the part—I'd know if I was going to be food for the "Mutant Martian."

"You sure this is the place?" Dad asked, as he peered through the windshield. He tried to sound stern and bored at the same time. That meant only one thing . . . he was excited. Really excited. (You'd have to know my Dad to know that's how he handles excitement. You'd also have to know that Mom had already spilled the beans by saying Dad had really bragged about me to his boss, the dreaded Mr. Feinstein.)

"Not bragged," Dad protested. "I just let him know that Wally here might be able to get him in to see some of the filming. Particularly the scenes with Laura Lottalips."

"Laura Lottalips is in the film?" I asked in surprise.

"Oh, I thought I told you." He pretended to yawn. "Yeah, Laura Lottalips, Bill Crimson, and what's that new, punk heart-throb all the girls are crazy over?"

"Steel," Mom jumped in, a little too quickly. "Chad Steel."

"Right," Dad said, throwing her a look. "Chad Steel."

"Chad Steel's in the film?" I cried. I couldn't believe my ears. Chad Steel was like the coolest guy in the world. He had this incredible hair, and everybody loved him, girls and guys both. I mean, he was what every guy wanted to be . . . and what every girl wanted every guy to be.

We pulled to a stop in front of the building. It was huge, and there were no windows—only an open door. And from that door, all sorts of eerie sparks and flashes could be seen. It was spooky—like maybe there was a real flying saucer inside . . . like maybe a real Martian swung by to audition for the part.

"Must be welding something," Dad noted.

So much for the Martian.

"Well," Dad sighed, again pretending to be bored, "let's see what these hot shots have in mind."

The three of us climbed out of the car and headed for the sparking and flashing light pouring from the door.

The closer we got, the more we heard the yelling . . . lots and lots of yelling:

"I've got deadlines! I've got schedules!" the voice shouted. This was followed by a bunch of swearing. "So you better *blank, blank* you lousy, *blank-blank* before I *blankety blank* your *blank blank.* We start in four days! Got it! Four (*a bunch more blanks*) days!

I threw a glance to Mom. She looked a little pale. Not me. I hear this sort of stuff every day. Of course, I never use it. That's one of the ways I let people know I'm a Christian. It's not a big deal, just kind of my way of saying I'm different and I'm gonna stay different and you're not going to make me undifferent.

Finally we arrived at the door. *Well, this is it,* I thought as we stepped inside.

The man doing all the blankety-blanking was standing and looking up at a giant . . . well, I can't explain it. It was like a giant, three-story steam shovel with all sorts of cables and steel mesh and hydraulic thingies that were hissing and clicking.

An operator stood on the floor in front of a giant control panel pushing levers and turning knobs. This made the thing toss what might have been its head and open and close what might have been its mouth. Other workers were scurrying around its feet (all three of them). They were stapling on a bunch of greenish rubber which suddenly made the feet look like they were alive.

The yelling man spotted us. "There you are," he glanced at his watch. "You're late."

"We thought we'd wait till the swearing slowed down," Dad answered pointedly.

All right! Two points, Dad.

"Sorry," the man said with a nod of apology to Mom and me. "We're just under a lot of pressure here." He turned from the hissing and clicking monster and headed for us. "I'm Bernard Elliott, director of this little disaster." He shook Dad's hand and then mine. His face suddenly had the same pasted-on smile as the lady at the audition. "And you must be Mr. Wally."

"Uh, McDoogle," I said, somehow feeling I'd had this conversation before.

But he didn't hear. He was too busy keeping up the fakey smile. "So . . . rumor has it you're quite a screamer."

"I guess," I shrugged. *I guess? What type of answer is that. Your entire future depends upon this one man's decision, and the best you can come up with is, "I guess?"*

"I hope you like heights," he chuckled as he looked back up to the monster's mouth. The operator moved the mechanical Martian's "jaws" back and forth as if it were chewing something.

"Heights?" I asked looking up to the massive mouth.

The director smiled. "If you're going to be bait for ol' Gertrude here, our little alien from Mars, you better be able to stand heights."

I continued to stare at Gertrude's mouth. "Sure," I kinda half croaked.

The director broke into a grin. "Welcome aboard, Son. You'll be fine for my picture, just fine."

It happened so quickly I couldn't tell for certain, but it sounded like I just got the part! Then suddenly ol' Gertrude started to hiss and click even louder.

The director spun around and shouted at the operator. "What's going on?"

The operator had no time to answer. The entire contraption was starting to shudder and rock. Desperately the man shoved the levers and turned the knobs. Nothing worked. Instead, the mouth chewed faster and faster, the neck started swaying back and forth.

The assistants at the feet quickly scattered. "Look out! She's going to blow again!"

A hose broke around in the creature's neck. Compressed air hissed from it! Then another hose broke. And another. Suddenly the entire monster began to vibrate. Then its head fell forward . . . as more hoses snapped and more air hissed.

The hissing air was deafening, but nothing compared to the director's shouting as he raced up to the operator and yelled right in his face. "Four days, Mister . . . Four *blankety, blank blank* days!"

We scrambled behind a van for safety and poked our heads out to watch. So this was the monster from Mars. So this was what was supposed to eat me.

Mom and Dad looked pretty skeptical. I knew it would take more than a little fast talking to convince them it would be okay, that everything would be safe. (Of course I'd have to convince myself, first.) But as far as the director was concerned, it sounded like I just got my first part in a movie.

As Gertrude rocked and hissed and swayed, I just hoped it wouldn't be my last.

Chapter 4

Death of a Dork-oid

It didn't take much talking to convince Dad to let me stay in the movie. (The guy was as excited about it as I was.) So we hung around and worked things out with the director. You know, the little details like money and the safety of my life—that sort of stuff.

Then it was home to bed and sleep. Well, sort of sleep.

I was scheduled to begin filming in two days! In a mere forty-eight hours I would be a star! Me and Chad Steel rubbing elbows! Hanging out. Swinging by and doing interviews with Phil Donahue, Oprah Winfrey, and Jay Leno.

Eventually I did drop off to sleep. But my dreams were so weird that I was more tired when I woke up than when I went to bed.

First there was Gertrude, the mechanical monster from Mars. As far as dreams about mechanical monsters go, she was pretty normal . . . well, except for the straw hat and tap shoes. She was doing a pretty good job of singing "Swanee River" . . . considering the breathtaking Melissa Sue Avarice was riding on top of her neck, waving a cowboy hat, and shouting "Yippie-I-O-Ki-Ay!"

Hey, I warned you it was weird. Unfortunately there was more . . .

Dad's boss, Mr. Feinstein, was standing on a fire-truck ladder shouting through a megaphone. "Action, Ms. Lottalips, I want action, action, action!" while super-hunk Chad Steel danced a ballet on the hood of the truck with Mom and Burt and Brock. (I'd never seen my brothers in tights. I hope I never have to again.) All this was happening as Opera crawled around on Gertrude's back with a magnifying glass shouting, "I found another flea, I found another flea! And, to top it off, Wall Street had me bound in chains like a slave and was auctioning me off to the highest bidder. (When I awoke, they were up to 29 cents.)

But that dream was nothing compared to the weirdness of the rest of my day.

First there was . . .

BREAKFAST WITH BROCK

"Hey, Squirt—you want a ride to school?"

"What?" I said, nearly choking on my Cheerios.

Burt and Brock never gave me the time of day . . .
unless it was to yell at me for using all the toilet
paper and not replacing it, or for leaning against
their precious cars or something important like
that. It's not that my brothers hated me. It's just,
well, since I didn't like sports, they figured I really
wasn't part of the family, so why get too attached.

He cleared his throat and repeated, "I said, do
you want me to take you to school?"

"Well . . . sure . . . " I cautiously answered. "What's
the catch?"

"No catch," he shrugged. "Valerie, my new babe,
wants to talk to you about breaking into the biz."

"Biz?" I asked.

"Yeah, you know, show biz . . . "

"Oh . . . sure, no sweat." But it was a sweat. I had
no idea what he was talking about.

Then there were . . .

DISCUSSIONS WITH DAD

"Don't forget to ask if Mr. Feinstein can visit the
set!" He chugged down the rest of his coffee and
pick up his briefcase. On his way to the door, he
sidestepped my sister's backpack and tripped over
our disaster-prone cat, Collision.

"No prob," I called from the kitchen. "Maybe I
can get Mr. Feinstein a love scene with Laura
Lottalips."

"Don't be smart. You know how important it is for me to make a good impression if I want to get that promotion."

I nodded. For years Dad had been trying to make a good impression and get that promotion. And for years Mr. Feinstein had been brain dead about what a great worker Dad was.

Then there was . . .

SOCIALIZING AT SCHOOL

Besides the usual gawks and winks and nods . . . which I was getting pretty used to, there was Wall Street. She had hired some sort of photographer guy who started firing off all sorts of pictures of me.

"Wally, meet Bruce."

I stuck out my hand. *FLASH* He took a picture.

"What's going on?" I asked Wall Street. *FLASH*.

"Thought we'd get some eight-by-tens of you— *FLASH* —so you can autograph them. *FLASH, FLASH*. Should get a couple bucks a piece off 'em if we're lucky. *FLASH, FLASH, FLASH*. You don't mind, do you?" *FLASH*

"No, of course not," I said as I stumbled up the school steps, totally blinded by the flashes.

Even Reptile Man was cool—well, as cool as a person like him can be.

"Wallace," he caught me as I headed past his

door. "Would it be, that is to say . . ." he pushed his glasses back up on his sweaty nose, " . . . about that mechanical monster they're using in the movie . . . the creature who's supposed to eat you . . . "

I looked at him, watching his twitching lips and the rivers of perspiration trickling over his brow.

"Do you suppose . . . that is to say . . . " he pushed his glasses up again, " . . . would it be possible for me to take a peek at it—for scientific purposes, you understand—to see how it operates?"

I couldn't believe it, even Reptile Man was asking for favors. I broke into a smile. "No sweat Repti . . . er Mr. Reptenson, I'm sure I can get you in to see it."

The corners of his twitching lips turned into a thin, sweaty smile. "Thank you, Wallace."

Unfortunately, there was one person who hadn't changed. And that brings us to the . . .

OPERATIONS OF OPERA

I mean, the guy still acted like we were best friends or something. Don't get me wrong, I still felt for him. But he had to understand I was different, now. It's true, at one time, I kinda liked being a Dork-oid (as if I had any choice). But things had changed. I had graduated. Now I was Wally McDoogle, superstar. I couldn't just hang out with anybody.

"Wally," he came up beside me as I headed down the hall.

"Now what?" I groaned so loud that I hoped he would get the message. No luck. He was just as friendly as ever.

"Reptile Man said the flea idea was cool. We can start it any time."

"What flea idea?" I said, acting as if he were barely there. If I treated him like scum maybe he'd get the idea.

"Our science project, remember?"

"Hey, Barker," I shouted over to one of the metal heads. "How's it goin', man?"

"Awesome, little buddy, outstandingly awesome."

We traded high fives as I continued down the hall.

Opera stayed glued to my side. He held up his match box. "I think one of the females is already starting to lay eggs," he proudly beamed.

That was it. I had tried everything I knew to get through to him in a nice way, and he still wouldn't take the hint. It was time to play hardball.

"Listen, Opera." I came to a stop and looked him squarely in the eyes. "Things have changed. I've got more important things on my mind. More important people to hang out with."

A look of hurt started filling his eyes. It killed

me, but I had to go on. "We're going to begin filming tomorrow, so I'd appreciate your not bothering
me anymore."

He just stared. Then blinked. I really ached for
him, but I pushed it aside. I had to. Otherwise I'd
fall right back into Dork-oidism.

I turned and headed down the hall.

A couple of popular girls were just ahead. "Hey,
Jill . . . Susie . . . wait up." I joined them, and
we all started joking and laughing. I threw a look
over my shoulder. I couldn't help myself. I guess I
still felt a lot for the guy.

He stood all alone. When he caught me looking,
he suddenly brightened. "Don't worry," he shouted,
"I understand."

It's about time.

"I'll work on the project by myself till you're
done. Then we'll get together . . . all right?"

I looked away.

"Just like old times! Dork-oids forever!" He held
up his fist and little finger in our secret sign.
"Right, Wally?"

My heart broke. I wanted to run back to him.
But I couldn't. I had to do this. I had to be free of
him. No matter what my heart felt. No matter
what that still small voice inside me said. I turned
and continued down the hall.

Finally, that afternoon there was . . .

MANEUVERS WITH MELISSA

"Hi, Wally."

I spun around. There she was in all her splendor. As usual, she was surrounded by her crowd of "Melissa Sue wanna-be's." Two per side. They were all popping and snapping their gum in perfect unison.

I knew it was my turn to say something, but at the moment nothing came to mind. At the moment, I wasn't even sure if I had a mind—just a whole herd of butterfly, all fluttering around my stomach at the same time.

I opened my mouth, hoping something would come out. Something smart. Something cool. Something to make her stand up and take notice.

"Hi," I squeaked back. Well, so much for smart, cool, and taking notice.

She gave me a pathetic smile. The kind you give wounded animals along the side of the road. "Listen," she asked, continuing to pop and snap her gum. "Do you, like, think you're gonna, like, get a chance to meet Chad Steel?"

A chicken would have lied. He would have said anything to impress her. So, of course, I did my best Kentucky Fried imitation. "Of course, I know Chad." Talk about being chicken. Any minute I figured I'd start clucking and laying eggs. I felt awful. I hated lying. But the way Melissa Sue's eyes widened in excitement, I knew more was coming. Sure enough. I opened my mouth and out popped, "Oh, yeah, me and Chad, we're like, buds."

"No way," she practically squealed.

"Oh, yeah. We go way back."

She grabbed my arm and sorta jumped up and down. I couldn't believe it, Melissa Sue was touching me. What next? Meeting her parents? Getting engaged? Picking out houses? "Do you think, like, maybe you could get me a lock of his fabulous hair?" she gasped.

"For you, Missy," I heard myself say, ". . . anything."

And then the most incredible thing happened. Something so surprising, so wonderful that it almost made the lie worthwhile . . .

Almost.

Melissa Sue Avarice was so excited that before I knew it she gave me a quick little peck on the cheek.

I was seeing stars . . .

I was hearing music . . .

I was in over my head. *Way over.* And I was getting in deeper by the second.

Chapter 5

Lights, Camera, Not So Much Action

Things were not well in McDoogleville—not well at all. Everything was too weird. I couldn't sleep. Nobody was acting like they were supposed to. I mean, think about it:

—My brother Brock pretends to like me . . .

—Dad uses me to impress his boss . . .

—Reptile Man treats me like a human being . . .

—Melissa Sue Avarice gives me a juicy smack in public . . .

I mean on the McDoogle Weirdness Scale of 1–10 this was definitely pushing an 11.

Then there was the way I treated Opera—like pond scum. It really bugged me. Amazing . . . one little part in one little movie and suddenly everybody goes schizoid on me. Everybody, including me!

I glanced at the clock. It was 12:24 in the morning. Tomorrow was Saturday. The big day. The day we'd begin filming. But I was too nervous to sleep. I reached for ol' Betsy and snapped her on. Maybe a little more James Brawn would help me relax. Let's see, where were we . . .

When we last left our super spy guy, he was in his Lear jet speeding toward the nation of Hollyweird. His mission: to rescue the world's TV commercials from the dreaded Lizard Lips. As the wind whips through his gorgeous hair (it's a convertible jet), James devises a plan. Since Lizzie is a three-hundred-foot-long lizard, chances are she'll be living in a three-hundred-foot-long lizard hole. Brilliant, huh? That's why they pay him the big, secret-agent bucks!

James reaches over and switches on his Handy-Dandy Lizard Hole Finder and:

Beep . . . Beep . . . Beep . . . BEEP-BOINK, BEEP-BOINK.

He finds it.
He down shifts his jet to "drop-like-

a-rock," and the plane nose dives toward the giant opening. "Strange," he
wonders, "why is this hole surrounded by
white, pearly boulders — white pearly
boulders that look exactly like —

"Leapin' Lima Beans!" he cries.
"They're teeth! Lizzie's got her mouth
open, and I'm headin' directly into —

But he has no time to finish the sentence. As he enters her mouth, he fires
an Emergency Dental Floss Missile. A
rocket attached to a thin white cord
shoots out from the back of the plane
and wraps itself around Lizzie's upper
bicuspid (that's a tooth for you non-
dentist types).

The cord yanks the jet to a screeching halt.

"Looks like it's time for a little
flossing," James laughs as he hops out.
But he doesn't laugh long. Now, I don't
want to say ol' Lizzie's breath is
bad . . . but there's something about
the way it melts all the plastic parts
on James' jet that makes our hero a
little nervous.

"Gotta lay off them onions, Babe!" he
shouts as he reaches into his shirt

pocket and pulls out a pencil. But this
is no ordinary pencil. Oh, no, dear
reader. He puts one end into his mouth
and starts blowing. The pencil inflates
into a giant bazooka — complete with
printed instructions in both French and
Chinese!

Next, he reaches into his back pocket
and pulls out the bottle of Listerine
that he keeps handy for just such oc-
casions. He loads it into the bazooka
and fires it directly into the back of
Lizzie's mouth.

It explodes, filling the reptile's
mouth with a fine mist of mouthwash. Now
the air is fit for human consumption.
A little mediciney perhaps, but for the
mouth of a giant lizard (they eat bugs
and that type of junk), it isn't half
bad.

Now, at last James can breathe. "Okay,
Lizzie girl," he shouts. "Where did you
hide those commercials?" But there is
still no answer, just the boiling and
bubbling of digestive juices from down
in her stomach.

James' keen eye keenly surveys his
not-so-keen situation...Ahead of him

are Lizzie's tonsils, throat, and past that what could be a bad case of indigestion...for both of them.

Behind him, closed tighter than the mouth of a three-year-old not wanting to eat his veggies, are the pearly teeth. But, at this range they're not so pearly. In fact, it looks like Lizzie girl has missed her last couple dental checkups...for the last couple centuries.

Knowing how sensitive actresses are about perfect smiles, James hates to do what he's about to do. But knowing he has to do what he has to do, he decides to do it...(or something like that).

He aims his handy-dandy laser ring (the prize from his Cracker Jack's box) at Lizzie's two front teeth. He's going to have to blast out a little escape route. Then, just when he's about to open fire and give her dental work some free air conditioning, he hears a giggle.

James quickly hits the deck (which just happens to be Lizzie's tongue), rolls onto his stomach, and takes aim...

"Don't shoot! It's me!"

James peers into the darkness. He sees nothing. "Who?"

"Me..." the voice giggles, "Poppin Fresh."

James watches in astonishment as the Pillsbury Doughboy jumps out from behind a left molar. Although worn and tattered, Poppin Fresh is just as white and pudgy as on TV. James has this sudden urge to poke him in the stomach (you know, just to see if he'll giggle like in the commercials). But he manages to keep from it.

"What are you doing here?" James demands.

"I'm hiding."

"Hiding?"

"Yes, Lizard Lips was holding me captive with all the other commercials until I made my escape."

"Listen," James says, "I know you're just a piece of cookie dough and not terribly bright, but there are safer places to hide than inside a giant lizard's —"

Suddenly Lizzie begins to speak. "Looksssss like I have you two

ssssssurrounded." Her voice roars in
their ears. "I trusssst you'll be
ssssstaying for lunch," she chuckles,
"ssssince you're the main coursssssse."
She begins laughing louder. And louder.
And louder still. The ol' girl is really cracking herself up. And the more
she laughs the wider her mouth opens,
until she provides the perfect escape
route.

"Let's go," James shouts to Poppin
Fresh. "Take me to the other prisoners."

Ol' Poppy boy gives a nervous look to
the towering incisors (more tooth talk)
high over their heads. One false move
and they'll wind up tooth tartar forever. But how can he be frightened
with the great James Brawn at his side?
Finally Poppin gives a nod. They leap
from the giant mouth and run for their
lives.

"Sssstop!" Lizzie screeches. "Sssssstop
it thissssss inssssstant!"

She flicks her forked tongue and takes
off after them when suddenly —

Suddenly, what? I wasn't sure. But something

inside said their fate wouldn't be any worse than
mine. I shut ol' Betsy down and glanced at the
clock—1:46 A.M. Five hours to go before I was on
the movie set. Five hours and then . . . well, your
guess is as good as mine. . . .

*   *   *   *   *

"Wally, the limo's here," Mom shouted from
downstairs. "Let's go, Sweetheart!"

Saturday morning . . . D-Day.

I glanced into my dresser mirror. I'd washed and
combed and sprayed and moussed my hair five different times, five different ways. And each time it
came out the same—wrong. I looked as close to
being a movie star as my pet turtle. (Which I don't
have because he was squished by a Volkswagen,
and we buried him over a year ago. By now he's
probably all rotten, and even at that, he probably
still looked better than me.)

Then there were my clothes . . . Every shirt
and pair of pants I ever owned were tossed on the
bed—well, except for the pair I decided to wear.
I knew plaid was no longer in style, but it was the
only thing I could find to wear with my polka-dot
shirt and striped suspenders. As strange as it
seems, some people claim I have no sense for
fashion.

"Sweetheart, hurry!"

"Well, here goes nothing," I sighed into the mirror. (I had no idea how right I'd be.)

I stumbled down the steps, and there was Mom. I couldn't believe it. It was 5:30 in the morning, and she was dressed and smiling! Little sister Carrie and her accident-prone kitty, Collision, were also up. Even Burt and Brock, the human sleeping machines, were awake! Granted, they weren't thinking yet (that doesn't start until five or six in the afternoon), but at least they were standing.

Meanwhile Dad was behind the video camera taping away. "Look this way, Son . . . give us a big smile."

"Nice 'do,'" Carrie smirked, checking out my hair. "Hope the monster'll still want to eat you."

I wanted to fire off a stinging comeback, but since the video was running, I played the "understanding big brother" and just patted her on the head.

By the time I reached the door, Mom was all in tears like I was going off to war. I wondered if she knew something I didn't.

Dad shouted from behind the camera, "Don't forget to get Mr. Feinstein on the set."

"Right," I nodded.

"And help Valerie get into the biz," Brock muttered.

"Got it," I answered. Then turning to Carrie I smirked. "What about you, don't you want anything out of me?"

She took a moment to think. Then, using all of her six-year-old wisdom she spoke, "Try not to make a total fool of yourself."

I nodded. Out of the mouths of babes . . .

Well, at least the fond farewells were over.

Not exactly.

I opened the front door and saw half the neighborhood standing on our front lawn! Many were still in their bathrobes. Several were half asleep. But as soon as they saw my face, they got all excited.

"There he is!" someone called.

"Wally's here!" another shouted.

"It's about time," someone mumbled.

They began to clap and cheer.

"Knock 'em dead," a neighbor cried.

"Do us proud," another shouted.

"Don't embarrass us," the mumbler mumbled.

The limo waited at the end of the sidewalk. It was long and black. The driver stood with the back door open. He was old and gray. "Right this way, Mr. Wally."

I stepped forward and climbed inside. I'd never seen anything like it. The seats were all leather. There was a telephone, a bar, a color TV, and, well talk about room . . . if it were any bigger I could have played a game of table tennis. Forget the table, I could of played real tennis!

The chauffeur shut the door. It went *"Wuff."* Not "Bang," not "Boom," not "Slam" . . . but *"Wuff."* Talk about class. There weren't even cookie crumbs or pop stains on the seat.

We pulled off as the crowd clapped and cheered. Mom was dabbing the corner of her eyes, Dad was video taping, Carrie was coaxing Collision out from under the rolling wheels, and Burt and Brock were dozing.

A half hour later we pulled onto the set. It was a fake city street. Oh, the fronts of the buildings looked real enough, but they had no backs. Come to think of it, they had no sides or floors or roofs either. They were just false fronts of buildings. Talk about fakey.

But they weren't the only fakey things . . .

The chauffeur opened the door, and I stepped out. Everybody was running around shouting. There was cable and lights and yelling everywhere. They probably all knew what they were doing, but they sure had me fooled.

Right above me towered ol' Gertrude—almost three-stories high. She didn't look like a machine anymore. Now her steel girders were completely covered with slippery, green rubber. Now she looked like a real monster—half dinosaur, half outer-space alien, half who-knows-what . . . complete with one giant red eye, four arms, three feet, and the obligatory drool hanging from her mouth.

"I'm supposed to get in there?" I kinda croaked as I pointed to the mouth.

But before the chauffeur could answer, two people grabbed me—a man and a woman (at the moment I couldn't tell which was which).

"You're late, Mr. Wally! We must get you into wardrobe immediately!"

"Oh, this hair is wrong," the other cried, running his (or her) hand through it. "Wrong, wrong, wrong. You don't look a thing like a Punker."

"A Punker?" I asked as they dragged me toward a trailer. "I thought the director hired me cause I looked like—"

"That was yesterday," the first sighed, "but today is today. You know artists . . . "

"You don't mind if we pierce your ears do you?" the first asked.

"Well, I—"

"Not a lot . . . Just four or five times . . . per ear."

"Well, I—"

"Where did you get these ghastly clothes?" the other cried, "Was Bozo the clown having a garage sale?"

"Well, I—"

Suddenly the sound of glass crashed and tinkled inside a nearby motor home. A voice screamed. "I'm not going near that machine! That's the stunt man's job!"

"But Chad, Sweetheart, Baby," another voice tried to reason, "We *need* those close ups."

There was another crash of glass. "And where's my Perrier—you promised me chilled Perrier!"

My first companion threw a glance over to the second. "Looks like Chaddy is having another one of his tizzy-fits," he (or she) smirked.

"Who?" I asked.

"Mr. Steel," the other answered, "the star of this little migraine maker."

"You don't mean *Chad Steel*?" I asked.

Before they could answer, the door to the motor home flew open and out stepped the director. He looked pretty worn and frazzled. In fact, he reminded me a lot of Carrie's cat, Collision, the time he got caught in the dryer. He had come out all wide-eyed, hair sticking out, and a little dazed.

Behind the director, stepped out Chad Steel. Well, it sort of looked like Chad Steel. Only this Chad Steel was about a foot shorter than I figured and twenty or thirty pounds wimpier.

"Look," the director pleaded. He pointed to the towering machine. Gertrude was tossing her head back and forth and moving her jaws like she was eating again. "All the bugs are worked out. See. She's perfectly safe, now. Perfectly."

"I can't see a thing," Chad whined. "The sun's too bright, it's hurting my—"

"Here," the director took off his sunglasses and handed them to Chad.

Unfortunately this was just about the time ol' Gertrude's mouth decided to hiccup. Well, that's how it started. But pretty soon it wasn't just her mouth hiccuping. Pretty soon it was her head, then her neck, then her entire body. Pretty soon the mechanical monster was jumping around like a kangaroo! A swaying, out-of-control, thirty-foot, hiccuping, kangaroo!

"Look out!" the crew yelled, running for cover. "She's going to blow again!"

And then, right on cue, Gertrude's head blew up. That's right. One minute she looked as normal as any other mutant monster from Mars—the next, her head blew up and there was nothing but steel girders, shredded rubber, and hanging wires.

"I want my manager," Chad shrieked. "I want my manager, and I want him now!"

"Good," my first wardrobe companion half laughed, half giggled. "Looks like we'll have more time to fix Mr. Wally."

"Hope you brought a book," the other sighed to me. "No way will we be filming today."

Chapter 6

A Day Off ... or an Off Day?

I spent the rest of "Superstardom: Day One" in the wardrobe trailer. It was hot and sticky and cramped. (Not exactly the type of glamor I was expecting.) With Gertrude on the fritz (not to mention Chad), we wouldn't start filming until Monday. But the man and woman (I still didn't know which was which) kept me around to try out a bunch of clothes and makeup. The clothes got weirder every second. By the end of the day they'd settled on a leather shirt and chiffon pants. I'd say that about covers it for weird, wouldn't you?

When I wasn't trying on clothes, I was trying out different rub-on tattoos for my arms, or begging them not to turn my ears into Swiss cheese with their ear-piercer thingie. They agreed to hold off with the ears till Monday.

They didn't agree to hold off with cutting and dying my hair . . .

The guy (or gal) began snipping as the other guy (or gal) tried red, then green, then purple, blue, orange. . . . We must have tried every color in the rainbow. And by the end of the day, that's exactly what I looked like—a spiked, punked, mohawked rainbow. "Don't worry," they said. "A little soap and water, it'll wash right out—same with those rub-on tattoos."

That's what they said as I climbed into the limo Saturday night.

But as I sat in church Sunday morning, I knew it wasn't so.

I've got to hand it to Pastor Bergman. He did a pretty good job of not staring. Well, okay, he stared, but at least his mouth didn't hang open. Well, at least it didn't hang open all the time. Only when his eyes scanned over to my section of the church—which for some reason seemed to be about every four or five seconds.

Then there was the rest of the congregation. I know they did their best to pay attention to the Pastor. But no matter how hard they tried, their eyes kept darting over to my "illustrated arms" and my "Technicolor, glow-in-the-dark, 'do.'"

Even with all that, the sermon was good. Too good. Pastor Bergman read something out of the New Testament about how we shouldn't treat some people as more important than others. . . .

"My dear brothers, you are believers in our glorious Lord Jesus Christ. So never think that some people are more important than others. Suppose someone comes into your church meeting wearing very nice clothes and a gold ring. At the same time a poor man comes in wearing old, dirty clothes. You show special attention to the one wearing nice clothes. You say, 'Please sit here in this good seat.' But you say to the poor man, 'Stand over there,' or 'Sit on the floor by my feet!' What are you doing? You are making some people more important than others. With evil thoughts you are deciding which person is better."

I was glad he wasn't talking about me. Who did I know that was all that rich? Come to think of it, who did I know that was all that poor?

Then I got to thinking about Melissa Sue Avarice and the way she'd been treating me, all special and everything—ever since I got a part in the movie. Come to think of it, she wasn't the only one who'd been treating me special. Everybody from Reptile Man to Brock to Wall Street . . . even Dad had been treating me special.

True, I wasn't rich, but wasn't being famous kind of the same thing? Weren't they getting all buddy-buddies with me for the same reason—'cause suddenly I was a "somebody?" I mean, they used to treat *Wally the Dork-oid* like a bad case of the flu. But now that I was *Wally the Superstar* I was everybody's friend.

The thought kinda made me mad. It's like they weren't treating me nice because of me—they were treating me nice because I had a part in the movie.

But I didn't get too worked up about how they were acting because pretty soon I got to thinking how I was acting. Not how I'd been acting toward them, but toward Opera.

Wasn't I kinda doing the same thing? Wasn't I treating Opera like one of those poor people Pastor Bergman was talking about? Oh, sure, he wasn't poor, at least when it came to money. But when it came to popularity Opera was flat broke.

And while we're on the subject, what about Melissa Sue? Wasn't I treating her special because she was rich—maybe not in money, but definitely in looks and popularity?

Pastor Bergman kept preaching, and I kept feeling more and more uncomfortable. It had nothing to do with the color of my hair or the tattoos on my arms. It had everything to do with that still small voice . . . That still small voice that kept saying something was wrong . . . That still small voice that kept getting louder and louder the more Pastor Bergman preached.

But it would take a lot more than a small voice to get me to change. Tomorrow was my big day. My real big day!

Chapter 7

And . . . Action!

"All right everybody settle in please. This is a take! Places, people! PLACES!" A little man with a big megaphone and an even bigger mouth marched back and forth behind the cameras shouting at everyone. "This is an expensive shot so let's get it right the first take! Heads up! Everybody look alive!"

I couldn't believe it. It had finally come. My big moment. It was Monday morning . . . a week later (It had taken a whole week to get Gertrude repaired) . . . and here we were about to film my famous scene.

I stood with two other actor kids (a guy and a girl) on the make-believe corner of the make-believe street in front of a make-believe billboard. Gertrude had been rolled behind the billboard out of sight. Chad and Laura Lottalips (who looked about twenty years older in person) sat in an idling convertible about a hundred feet away.

We were all set. If everything went right, the scene would go like this:

There would be a big flash of light behind the billboard. That would be the Martian spaceship landing. Next, Gertrude would crash through the sign and grab me in her mouth. I would scream as the other two kids ran off. Gertrude would grab me in her mouth, start to raise me in the air, and then, at the last minute, Chad would race to my rescue in his fancy convertible.

"Couldn't be simpler," the director assured us. "If everything goes right, we'll have you out of here by noon."

"Noon of what day?" the boy actor smirked.

"Of what month?" the girl actor double smirked.

Both of the actors were from Hollywood (which probably explains the smirking). The guy was a big star in a big TV sitcom a couple years back. But that was a couple years back, so now no one knew who he was anymore.

And the girl? She was somebody's niece.

An hour earlier I had been yanked out of the limo by the makeup and wardrobe man and woman (I still didn't know which was which). We took exactly two steps before the director spotted us and shouted, "What the *blankety-blank-blank*

did you do with his *blankety blank blankety* hair,
you *blankety blank blank blanks!*" (The guy must
have been nervous. His blanks were in rare form
that morning.)

"You said you wanted a Punker," the first man
(or woman) explained.

"That was Saturday before last!" the director
cried. "Today Punk is out! Geek is in!"

"Of course, Bernie, anything you say, Bernie,"
the second man (or woman) apologized.

"Until I know what kind of movie I'm making, I
expect you to be flexible!"

"Our mistake Bernie," the first man (or woman)
said, "we should have known better." They rushed
me back to the trailer muttering a few of their own
blankety-blanks at the director.

"What does he mean, he doesn't know what type
of movie he's making?" I asked.

"The poor slob hasn't found the theme," the first
man (or woman) answered. "He has no vision for
the film, no handle, no statement . . . not yet, anyway."

"Well, when will he?" I asked.

"Soon," the second man (or woman) sighed. "We
hope very, very soon."

After an hour of trying on wigs, smearing makeup
all over my rub-on tattoos to cover them, and putting
me back in my regular clothes, I suddenly looked

like . . . well, after all that hard work, I wound up looking exactly like me.

Amazing. No wonder these people make so much money.

So, there I was Wally McDoogle, "All-American Geek," standing on the corner playing . . . well, playing Wally McDoogle, "All American Geek."

"Stand by!" the voice through the megaphone shouted.

This was it. All of the days of preparation; all of the hassles at school, at home, with my friends— it all came down to this moment of glory. In a matter of seconds I would be immortalized forever. I took a deep breath. I'd been practicing my scream for days. I had it down pat. True, I'd been getting a little hoarse lately, but that was okay. One healthy scream is all it would take.

Everybody waited:

—Gertrude as the monster behind the billboard.

—Chad and Laura Lottalips as the heroes in the convertible.

—And me, Wally McDoogle, as the monster bait.

"SOUND?" the megaphone man shouted.
"Speed!" someone called back.
"CAMERA?"

"Rolling," the man behind the camera yelled. SLATE IT!"

Another guy with a little blackboard cut in half raced in and shouted, "58-C, Take One!" He slapped the two pieces of wood together with a loud *CLAP,* then disappeared as quickly as he had appeared.

"AND . . . *ACTION!*" the director yelled.

It was now or never. I took a deep breath and let out the world's longest and loudest scream. It was unbelievable. I mean if they had Olympic events for screaming I would have picked up the Bronze, Silver, *and* Gold Metals.

"AHHHHHHHHHHHHHHHHHHHHHHHH HHHHHHHHHHHHHHHHHHHH . . ." I was amazing. I was incredible. I was about to pass out when suddenly the director screamed, "CUT!"

I looked around grinning, pretty pleased with myself. . . . Until the director stomped up to me and roared right into my face, "WHAT THE *BLANKETY BLANK* DO YOU THINK YOU'RE DOING? YOU DON'T *BLANK BLANK* SCREAM WHEN I SAY *BLANK BLANK* 'ACTION!' YOU SCREAM WHEN THE *BLANK BLANK* MON-STER BREAKS THROUGH THE *BLANK BLANK* BILLBOARD!"

"Oh," I sorta squeaked, "sorry." I know I could have had better comebacks, but when a man is

throwing those kinds of words right in your face,
it's pretty hard to think of anything too witty.
Besides he had a point. I wasn't supposed to
scream until *after* Gertrude broke through the
billboard.

"Okay," the director shouted as he turned and
headed back behind the camera. "Let's get it right
this time!"

"Okay," the little man with the big megaphone
shouted. "Let's get it right this time!"

The director crawled back onto his chair and
nodded.

Megaphone Mouth shouted, "Stand by people,
this is a take! SOUND?" he shouted.

"Speed!" came the answer.

"CAMERA?"

"Rolling!"

The man with clapboard raced in, "58-C, Take
Two!" He said, clapping the board and disappearing again.

"And . . . ACTION!" the director yelled.

This time I kept my mouth shut. No way would
I scream until Gertrude broke through the billboard.

There was a bright flash of light behind the sign
just like there was supposed to be.

"What was that?" the boy actor cried.

"Don't worry," I reassured him, "that's just the

special effects people. Remember there's supposed to be a flash behind the billboard and then—"

"CUT!"

Everyone was silent. Real silent. And everyone was staring . . . at me.

"What'd I do now?" I croaked.

"That's my line, stupid," the boy actor sneered.

"What?" My heart was somewhere in my throat with the sneaking suspicion that I'd messed up again.

"I'm *supposed* to say, 'What's that?'" the boy scoffed. "It's in the script."

I threw a look over to the director. He was *not* smiling—in a big way. Come to think of it, he was barely breathing. But he was glaring. Right at me. Hard. Real, real hard.

"Sorry," I shrugged giving him my famous McDoogle-the-idiot grin.

But he still wasn't smiling . . . even harder. At last he spoke. His voice was flat and calm and even . . . well, except for the slight quivering which let you know he was about to explode. "Let's set it up and try it again . . . "

TAKE THREE

Once again they all did their shouting routine:

"Sound?" *"Speed."* "Camera?" *"Rolling."* "Take three," "and . . . Action."

Once again there was a bright flash.

"What's that?" the boy actor shouted.

This time I kept my mouth shut.

"Look out!" the girl cried as she pointed to the billboard. "Gertrude's hit the sign—it's falling!"

The two actors sprinted out of the way leaving me standing there all alone. I didn't remember that being in the script, but I wasn't about to move. No sir. I'd learned my lesson. I just stood there waiting for my cue to scream—waiting for Gertrude to crash through the sign.

"RUN, YOU MORON!" the director shouted. "GET OUT OF THE WAY!"

I just blinked at him. No way was I going to make the same mistake twice. That is, until a stunt man rushed in, tackled me to the ground and rolled us out of the way . . . just as the billboard crashed to the ground right where I was standing."

I scrambled to my feet and cried. "What are you doing? That's not in the script!"

"Neither is that billboard falling," the stunt man chuckled, as he got up and brushed himself off.

Once the scare was over, it was chuckles all around. Everybody had a good laugh (except the director). I tell you, it felt kind of good hearing laughter again. It felt even better knowing I was the source of that laughter, kinda like being back

home, or at school, or anywhere else I ever went in
my life.

It took almost an hour for them to fix the billboard, and then we were ready for . . .

TAKE FOUR
Everything went perfect. The kids gave their
lines. I kept my mouth shut. And Gertrude's face
crashed through the sign just like it was supposed
to. It was a little scary having it come right at me,
but I could see the man at the control panel off to
the side. He pulled back the lever, and Gertrude
opened her mouth. He pushed another lever, and
she scooted toward me.

Now it was scream time. I took a deep breath
and let loose AHHHHHhhhhhhhh!" It was a little
weak and a little hoarse. But no one noticed because suddenly there was that famous, "CUT!"
again. Only this time it didn't come from the
director.

"WHO SHOUTED 'CUT'?" the director bel-
lowed. "THIS IS MY MOVIE, AND NOBODY
SAYS 'CUT' BUT ME! *WHO SAID 'CUT'?*"

"I did," Chad whined from his convertible. "I'm
out of eye drops! Without my eye drops, my eyes
will be all red and icky for the close-ups."

The veins in the director's neck began pumping
overtime. It looked like he was about to pop a

vessel . . . or two. I expected him to go into cardiac
arrest any second or at least to let loose with a
string of blankety blanks. But neither happened.
Instead, the director said just as softly as possible
(which made it even scarier), "Could someone
please bring Mr. Steel his eye drops?"

TAKE FIVE

They patched up the billboard and started
again. Everything went perfect. Gertrude crashed
through again, and I screamed. "AHHhhhh." It
was pretty pathetic, my voice was definitely going,
but no one cared. They just wanted to get the
scene done. Chad threw his car into gear and
raced up to me, when suddenly . . . you guessed it:

"CUT!"

"What is it now?" The director's voice trembled
in rage.

"My hair's all mussed," Laura Lottalips complained. "The wind's mussed my hair."

It was pretty obvious that Laura was lying. Her
hair was in perfect shape. She just wanted to say
"Cut" because Chad got to say "Cut." Suddenly, I
felt like I was back in kindergarten again. I mean
these guys were supposed to be grownups, right?
What was next? Somebody yelling "Cut" 'cause
they didn't have their Teddy?

TAKE SIX

"Ahhh . . . " My scream was so faint you could barely here it. But it didn't matter.

"CUT!"

This time we stopped because of Chad's makeup. It was almost noon, and the heat had made his "tan" (which was really lots and lots of brown body makeup) start to run. They hooked up a long hose to some inside air conditioner and ran it all the way out to Chad's car. Someone held it in front of him the whole time so he'd stay cool.

Which wasn't very long because someone else suddenly shouted, "LUNCH!"

Just like that, everybody turned and headed to the nearby tables that were set up. It looked like the director wanted to go on, like he still wanted to film, like he still had plenty of blankety blanks ready for anyone who wanted to listen. But no one seemed in the mood. Everyone was too hot and tired and cranky.

Later as I stood in line for the food, I was beginning to think maybe movie making wasn't as much fun as everyone thought. Maybe it was actually a lot of hard work. Maybe it was actually a lot of long, boring, get-used-to-people-screaming, monotonous, boring, get-used-to-people-screaming-evenmore, boring, hard work. Yes, sir, this movie-making stuff was about as glamorous as a bad case of athlete's foot. If the kids at school could see me now . . .

Kids at school! Leaping Lizards!

I was supposed to get Melissa Sue a lock of Chad's hair!

I was supposed to get Reptile Man in to see Gertrude!

I was supposed to get Dad's boss in to see Laura Lottalips!

And what about Brock's girlfriend?

I threw a look over to Chad. There were about a dozen people surrounding him as he headed off to his trailer—somebody wanted to do his nails; somebody wanted to touch up his makeup, his wardrobe, his eyes, and, of course, his magnificent hair. No way could I get to him. And no way did I *want* to get to him.

Then there was Laura. Ditto with her surrounding crowd. And ditto times two with my desire to talk to her.

Well, at least I could get Brock's girl, Reptile Man and Dad's boss onto the set. All I had to do was ask the director if . . .

"What the *blank blank* are those *blank blank* clouds doing up there?"

I looked over to the director. He was staring up at the sky.

"I can't have clouds in my shot. I want those clouds out of here and I want them out of here now!"

"But Bernie," the man with the megaphone tried to reason. "We can't control the clouds. The weatherman said it was supposed to rain this afternoon. We—"

"Rain? I can't have *blankety blank* rain in my shot!"

"Bernie, please."

"I don't want rain!"

"Bernie . . ."

"If you don't move those *blank blankety* clouds, I won't shoot the *blank blankety* scene today!"

"Bernie, be reasonable."

But Bernie wasn't reasonable. And a half hour later, I was in my limo heading to school. It was only 12:30 P.M., and they figured I could squeeze in half a day of classes. Believe it or not, I was looking forward to it. How nice it would be to be back in school with sane, normal people again.

Or would it? . . .

Chapter 8

The Plot Sickens

I knew I was in trouble the minute the limo pulled up to the school and I saw Wall Street selling my photos on the front lawn.

"Step right up," she yelled, waving my glossy, eight-by-ten-inch black and whites in the air. "Get your Wally McDoogle souvenir photos, only $10.95! Or get the entire collector's series for just $39.95. This special offer not available in stores. Visa and Mastercard are accepted!" (Ever get the feeling your friends watch too much TV?)

What was even more shocking were the dozens of kids waiting in line to buy those photos!

I climbed out of the car as discretely as possible. But being discrete is a little difficult when the car happens to be a big, black, shiny limo.

"There he is!" someone shouted. And before I knew it they were all running at me.

Now, the way I figured it, I had three choices:

A. Stand calmly and be trampled to death.
B. Walk calmly and be trampled to death.
C. Run like crazy for my very life.

It was a tough decision, but since I still had a thing for living, I chose C. I ran like a madman toward what I hoped would be safety inside the school.

But indoors wasn't much better.

"Why, Wallace, it's so good to see you." It was Reptile Man. He was doing another imitation of a grin. I looked up and returned the smile. I couldn't help myself. It was so good to see an everyday, normal person again. (Even though this particular everyday, normal person sweated like a lawn sprinkler.)

"You're just in time," he kept on trying to grin. I think the local TV cable crew is still here."

"TV crew?" I whispered hoarsely. Whatever voice I had was gone from all the screaming earlier that morning.

"Yes . . . they're in the gym with Opera's and your science project. Come along." He rested his clammy hand on my shoulder as we started down the hall. I could feel the dampness of his palms soak through my shirt. I remembered something about a science project, but what did he mean by TV crew?

"Hey, Wally, my man," someone shouted. "How's it going?"

Others followed suit. And before I knew it, there was an entire crowd following us down the hall.

"So . . . " Reptile Man said as he led me through the hall, "did you talk to the movie people into letting me see their mechanical monster?"

"Why, uh, . . . er . . . " I tried to give an answer that would keep Reptile Man smiling but that wasn't a lie. "No problem . . . Mr. Reptenson. Just, uh, show up. I'm sure you'll see it. (Hey, it wasn't a lie. It was so big, he couldn't miss it. Maybe he'd have to see it from a mile away, but at least he'd see it).

It worked. He broke into an even bigger attempt of a grin.

"Wally?" It was Melissa Sue Avarice in all of her perfect perfection. Perfect smile, perfect teeth, perfect . . . well, you get the picture. "Did you get a lock Chad Steel's hair for me?"

"I'm sorry," I rasped hoarsely. "With all of today's work I didn't get a chance."

Her perfect smile vanished. I knew I had to do something. I couldn't just break her heart (let alone, have it hate me). I'd given Reptile Man a half truth, and he bought it. Maybe I could do the same with Missy.

"Listen," I continued, "why don't you swing by

tomorrow. Maybe I could set up a meeting."
(Again, it wasn't a lie. I COULD set up a meeting.
Maybe not with Chad, but I could set up a meet-
ing with somebody . . . somewhere . . . sometime.)
Besides, what did I have to worry about? Neither
Missy nor Reptile Man would show up tomorrow.
It was Tuesday. They had school. I was covered. No
problem.

Well, except for that still small voice. It grew
louder every time I opened my mouth

We pushed open the gym doors. Lots of kids
milled around setting up their science projects.
Lots of kids including Opera . . . and the TV crew
that followed him around.

"There he is now!" someone shouted. "There's
Wally McDoogle!"

Everyone turned to me, including the TV crew.

"Hey, Wally!" Opera shouted. "You're just in
time."

The crowd kinda parted, and I made my way up
to a giant display all about fleas. It was incredible—detailed drawings of fleas, electron micro-
scope photographs of fleas, a clear plastic dome
with a magnifying glass so you could see the
fleas—I mean Opera had really knocked himself
out.

"And you boys built this yourself?" a reporter
asked, suddenly shoving a microphone into my face.

"We sure did," Opera interrupted, giving me a look that said play along with this. "Just the two of us, right, Wally?"

"Amazing," the reporter replied. "Not only is he our local celebrity, but he is a scientific whiz kid, as well."

Opera threw his arm around me. "You bet," he grinned toward the camera. "Wally's one talented dude . . . and my best friend."

Opera didn't have a selfish bone in his body. But for some reason, at that exact moment I thought he was using me. Just like everybody else. Just like Melissa, just like Reptile Man, just like everyone. By getting on TV, by claiming to be my friend, I thought Opera was using me to rise from his lowly Dork-oid state.

But what if the opposite happened? What if people saw us together and thought I'd slipped back into Dork-oid-hood? If that happened, I'd be right back where I started.

Before I knew it, I was squirming out from under Opera's arm. "I don't know what you're talking about." I said.

A look of concern shot through Opera's eyes.

"This isn't my project—I had nothing to do with it."

"Wally," Opera tried to keep smiling while talking through clenched teeth, "what are you talking

about? This is the science project that we all have
to do, that I agreed to help you with until—"

"I barely know him," I said turning to the reporter. "I mean we're in science class together and
everything. And we used to be friends and
stuff . . . but that was a long time ago."

"Wally . . . " I could hear the shock in Opera's
voice, but I couldn't look at him.

"A long, long time ago," I repeated just to make
sure no one missed my meaning. There, it was
done. I'd said it. I felt like dog drool, but at least I
had made my point.

"But he'll still be going with the rest of your
class to visit the set tomorrow, won't he?"

The reporter's question hit me like a ton of
bricks. "WHAT?" I half croaked/half screamed.

"The field trip Vice Principal Watkins set up for
tomorrow. He'll still be going on that."

"Mr. Watkins set up a field trip?" I sputtered
" . . . for our class? . . . to visit the set?"

"That's right. Tomorrow morning! I bet it'll be a
thrill for you to perform in front of your classmates, won't it?"

"More than you can imagine," I muttered in a
half daze. They asked me a bunch more questions
about being a star and working with Chad Steel
and Laura and all of that. But my head was too

busy spinning with all the promises I had made to Melissa and Reptile Man and everyone. If they were actually going to be on the set, how was I going to pull it off?

Then there was Opera. My one-time best friend. I glanced over to him a moment. That was all it took. My heart broke. He looked like somebody had punched him in the gut. Like his best friend had suddenly become a Judas.

. . . Maybe I had.

* * * * *

That night everybody made a big deal about watching me on TV and about the field trip Mr. Watkins had arranged. Brock's girlfriend just happened to swing by to say "hi." (What a coincidence.) Dad's boss just happened to call offering to "chaperone" the class tomorrow. (What a guy.) And Mom and Dad thought it would be a thrill to swing by and watch me work. (What fun.)

By the time my face flickered on the tube, I had sort of wandered out of the room.

"Come on, Sweetheart," Mom shouted. "You're missing it."

That was the whole idea. I was still bugged about Opera. Well, not about Opera but about me.

I had betrayed my best friend once that afternoon.
I wasn't in the mood to see an instant replay of it
that night.

I trudged upstairs to my room. With any luck,
tomorrow would be my last day of filming. With
any luck this whole awful business would be over.
People would stop using me, and I would stop
hurting them.

I reached for ol' Betsy and flipped her on. Maybe
James Brawn would have some answers . . .

The chase music blares loudly as James
and Poppin Fresh Dough race through the
desert from (Da-da-daaaa!—that's bad-
guy music) Lizard Lips. James is in
perfect shape and races like the wind.
(He has to. He's our hero.) Poppin
Fresh, on the other hand, is a bit over-
fed, and usually weighs in on the
"what's-that-hanging-over-your-belt"
side of the scales.

Poppin tries to speak, "Go ahead
(gasp, gasp) without me (wheeze,
wheeze). I can't (gasp, wheeze) make it
(wheeze, gasp)."

"Nonsense," James chuckles with
superior, super spy superiority. He

bends down and rips off his left shoe. He tears away the heel to reveal a hidden TV remote control.

"What are you doing?" Poppin pants.

James points the remote control at Lizzie, who is just a few hundred feet behind them. He presses the "Pause" button, and immediately Ms. Lips freezes in mid air.

"How'd you—"

"She's a TV character isn't she?" James asks.

"Well, yeah, but—"

"So she has to play by TV rules." Again James grins his great, good-guy grin. Now he points the remote at Poppin Fresh.

"What are you doing?" Poppin cries.

"You're a TV character, too, and we've gotta pick up the pace so..." He presses "Fast Forward." Suddenly Poppin Fresh is running faster than the nose of a kid with a bad cold.

Then James stops. He strains to listen. "Do you hear that?" he asks.

"It's the other prisoners," Poppin shouts.

Immediately, James presses "Volume" on

the remote control. The sound grows
louder. Now he can tell where they are.
"This way," he cries as they race toward a conveniently placed, nearby cave.

They dash inside the cold cavern and
come to a stop. Sure enough, there they
are — all the TV commercials — all locked
up together as prisoners. And they are
not happy... not happy at all.

To the left, the Keebler Elves are
arguing fiercely with the Double Mint
Twins. Not far away the Energizer Rabbit
is having an endurance contest with
the Duracell Dancers. Nearby, Tony the
Tiger is wrestling the Trix rabbit for
best two out of three falls as Cap'n
Crunch waits to take on the winner.

"What's going on?" James shouts to the
nearby Little Caesar's Pizza man dressed
in his Little Caesar's Pizza toga.

"Pizza, pizza," the little guy
shouts.

"No, I'm asking you—"

"Pizza, pizza!

"I don't want any—"

"Pizza, pizza!"

"Will you stop it with the—"

"Pizza, pizza!"

Our super spy is getting super
steamed. He turns to Colonel Sanders.
But the old-timer is trying to get a
hammerlock on Ronald McDonald. Then
there are those red spots from the
Seven-Up cans. They're bouncing all over
the place.

"This is crazy!" James yells.

"You know how competitive we are,"
Poppin Fresh shouts. "Put us in the same
room together, and we've just got to
beat the other guy. It's our nature."

"But your real enemy's outside. Any
second the batteries in my remote control will wear down, Lizard Lips will
unfreeze, and—"

"Too late, Jamesssssss."

Our hero spins around to see ol'
Lizzie slithering toward the cave. He
turns to the crowd and shouts, "Everybody, listen up! Listen up!"

But before he can say anything more,
James is suddenly trampled to the ground
by a dozen basketball stars racing each
other in "new and improved" basketball
shoes that they're all trying to sell.

"James . . ." Poppin cries, as he runs
to him. "James, can you hear me?"

But James does not answer. He lies on
the ground unconscious.

"What'ssss the matter?" Lizard Lips
hisses as she closes in. "Did Jimmy Boy
fall down and go boom?" Once again she
begins laughing her sinister lizard
laugh. Once again things look impossibly hopeless for our impossibly
good-looking secret agent when suddenly—

I came to a stop. I had no *suddenly's* left . . . in
either this story or my life. My situation was just
as hopeless as James Brawn's. Well, tomorrow it
would all be over. I'd play the superstar for everybody one last time, and then things would finally
get back to normal. Right?

Then, again . . .

Chapter 9

Send in the Fleas!

The next day the limo dropped me off at the movie set bright and early. If I was a *little* lucky, we'd finish before my class ever showed up. If I was *a lot* lucky, there'd be a major earthquake, and the ground would open up and swallow me whole.

Unfortunately, it was not my lucky day . . .

First, it took a couple hours to get Gertrude working right. She was hiccuping again. Then a couple more hours to get Chad out of his dressing room. He was whining again—something about a pimple that he didn't want his "public" to see.

Anyway it was 11:00 by the time we were all in our places. Me, my actor buddies, Chad, Laura, Gertrude, the billboard, the convertible, . . . oh, and about a hundred of my so-called "fans." They had all shown up and were standing behind a roped off area gawking at me.

A lot of them—like Reptile Man, Melissa Sue, Brock's girlfriend, and Dad's boss—were waiting for me to make good all of my hotshot promises. Others, like Opera (who was carrying around a giant shoe box full of our newly hatched fleas), were there simply to watch and cheer me on.

"Atta boy, Wally!" someone yelled from behind the rope.

"Do us proud," Dad called from behind his video camera.

"If you die, can I have your computer?" Wall Street shouted.

"Quiet!" the little man with the big megaphone cried. "Quiet, or you'll have to clear the set."

They all settled down and waited.

It was kinda cool having everyone watch me. I'd be lying if I said it didn't feel good. I'd also be lying if I said it was worth all the pain and hassles I'd been through. With any luck, it would be over in just two minutes. Then again, we've already talked about my luck . . .

They went through the usual shouting countdown of "Sound?" . . . *"Speed."* . . . "Camera?" . . . *"Rolling."* . . . until we finally came to, "And . . . ACTION!" Everybody remembered what to do. Everything went like clockwork. Well, for a second . . .

Once again there was the flash behind the billboard.

Once again my actor buddy cried, "What's that!"

Once again Gertrude's head crashed through the sign.

And, once again, I opened my mouth to scream. But before any sound came out, Gertrude started bucking. I threw a look over to her operator at the control panel. He had that same, "*UH-OH, NOW WHAT?*" look on his face. Before I could jump back Gertrude opened her jaws and grabbed my left leg.

Then things really went haywire!

We all knew Gertrude was supposed to pick me up—it was in the script. But not like this. She wasn't supposed to pick me up by my left leg. We weren't supposed to go shooting up into the air quite so high or quite so fast. And her body was not supposed to bounce and buck out of control.

But it did.

The crowd gasped. Well, everyone but Dad. "Relax," he said, smiling from behind his video camera, "I talked to the director, it's all in the script, it's perfectly safe."

Not quite . . .

I was dangling thirty feet in the air, hanging by one foot from Gertrude's mouth. All this as she did the two-step or hokey-pokey or whatever dance routine she was learning. With every buck and hop, my foot sipped further and further out of her mouth. With every buck and hop I was coming closer and closer to a little one-on-one, face-to-face

chat with God. Now being the cool, calm professional I am, I did what any cool, calm professional
would do. I screamed for my Mommy!

"MOMMMM . . . (bounce, buck) DAD . . .
(buck, bounce) SOMEBODY GET ME (bounce,
buck, buck, bounce) DOWN FROM HERE!"

I caught a glimpse of Gertrude's controller. He
was spinning dials and pulling levers, but he could
have been on a cruise to Tahiti for all the good he
was doing.

By now the entire film crew was in a panic.
Everyone but the director. "KEEP IT ROLLING!
he shouted to his cameraman, "KEEP IT ROLL-
ING!"

"See," Dad said a little less confidently, "they
know what they're doing."

"GET ME DOWN!" I kept screaming, "GET ME
DOWN FROM HERE!"

Reptile Man was the first to act. "It's a short!" he
shouted as he pushed his way to the front of the
crowd. He darted under the rope and started for
Gertrude's operator. A security guy tried to stop
him, but it did no good. "It's an electrical short in
your power convertor," he cried, as he finally broke
free and raced toward Gertrude's operator and
control panel.

"GET ME DOWN FROM HERE! GET ME
DOWN!"

"WALLY! WALLY!" Opera was also squirming and wiggling his way to the front of the crowd.

"KEEP IT ROLLING! KEEP IT ROLLING!" the director cried.

Reptile Man arrived beside Gertrude's operator and did what any scientifically trained, electronic genius would do. He gave the control panel a good solid kick.

Gertrude let out a hiss of gas as her neck dropped toward the ground. The only problem was, we were dropping at about a billion miles per hour!

"WALLY! WALLY!" It was Opera's turn to duck under the rope. He broke past the guard and raced toward us.

Even as I was about to die, I was impressed by Opera's love for me. Funny, after all I had done to him, he still cared. He was still trying to help. Not that there was a lot he and his giant "flea motel" could do . . . Still, when he finally joined me in heaven, I'd have to look him up and say "thanks."

In short, there was nothing anybody could do. Well, except for the director. But he knew a good scene when he saw one. "KEEP IT ROLLING! KEEP IT ROLLING!"

Then just before ol' Gertrude made me a permanent part of the pavement, Reptile Man gave her controls one last kick. She screeched to a halt just

a couple feet from the ground. Talk about close!
Then her mouth hissed open, and she spit me out.

"OH, WALLY, WALLY!" Opera shouted as he
raced toward me, all 187 pounds worth. He spread
open his arms as he ran at me, "YOU'RE SAFE!
YOU'RE SAFE!"

At the speed he was going, I knew I wouldn't be
safe for long. He hit me so hard that he knocked
me to the ground, and I rolled out of Gertrude's
reach.

Unfortunately, Opera didn't.

Suddenly ol' Gertrude let out another hiss.
Her mouth fell to the pavement and clanged
shut again. Only this time it was around Opera.

"AHHHHHHHHHHHHHHHHHHHHHHHHHHHH
HHHHhhhhhhhhhhhhhhhhhhhhhhhhhhhhhhhhh
hhhhhhhhhhhhhhh!" Opera screamed about a
hundred times better than I ever had.

"KEEP ROLLING," the director cried. "GO IN
FOR A CLOSE-UP! GO IN FOR A CLOSE-UP!"

The cameraman obeyed as Gertrude's head
again flew back up into the sky. Once again she
started bucking and bouncing her fancy dance.

Reptile Man dropped to his knees and, with the
operator's help, madly unscrewed the front of the
control panel.

The crowd screamed louder and louder.

"THIS IS GREAT!" the director cried. "CUE

THE CONVERTIBLE! CHAD, LAURA GET IN THERE FOR THE RESCUE!"

Chad nodded and threw his speedster in gear. It roared forward and squealed to a stop directly under Opera, directly under the bucking Gertrude.

Opera continued his scream, "AHHHHHHHHH HHHHHHHHHHHHHHHHhhhhhhhhhhhhhhhhhh hhhhhhhhhhhhhhhhhhhhhhhhhhhhhhhhhhhhh hhhhhhhhhhhhhhhhhhhhhhhh." (He seemed to be getting better with every breath.) But Opera wasn't just screaming for his life. There was something else at stake. For every time Gertrude bucked and jerked, she loosened Opera's hold on his shoe box. Try as he might, the big guy could no longer hold on. At last the box slipped from his hands. His prized possession, his family of one million newly hatched little pets plummeted toward the earth.

"MY FLEAS!" he screamed. It was like slow motion. Everyone watched his box tumble end over end. Everyone gasped as the lid gently came off and fluttered away. Everyone shrieked as the million fleas started raining down upon them.

Everyone but the director. "KEEP ROLLING! KEEP IT ROLLING!"

Laura Lottalips was the first to lose control. "GET 'EM OFF! GET 'EM OFF!" she screamed as the fleas showered over her. She slapped her shoulders and clawed at her hair. "SOMEBODY GET 'EM OFF!"

Now Chad would have been the likely volunteer, but he was too busy screaming his own brand of hysteria and tearing at his own hair . . . that is until he accidentally ripped off his toupee. That's right, Chad Steel's beautiful hair was nothing more than a wig. A major wig. Now everyone, including the camera, saw him for what he really was. Not the handsome middle-twenties hunk that set every heart a twitter. No, this was the older, nearly bald, coward that made everyone in the crowd start to boo.

Everyone but Dad's boss. In a flash Mr. Feinstein broke through the line shouting, "I'm coming, Laura; I'm coming." Before anyone could stop him, he had reached his dream of dreams, he had and come to her rescue. "I'm here, Ms. Lottalips, take my coat, there you go, atta girl." He wrapped his coat around the sobbing woman and helped her hobble off the set. It was a sight to behold. All that was missing was his suit of armor and white horse.

Meanwhile Reptile Man had torn away the cover of the control panel and ripped out a couple wires. Immediately, Gertrude stopped bucking— just like that. Amazing. Then Reptile Man turned another knob. There was the hiss of gas escaping as Gertrude slowly lowered Opera to the ground.

I threw a look over to the director. For the first time in the entire film, he was actually smiling. I couldn't believe it.

"And . . . Cut! Print it!" He said as he turned to his crew beaming. "We got it boys, we got ourselves the take!"

The crew broke into cheers and applause. Soon they swarmed around Opera slapping him on the back, telling him what a great job he did, what a great scream he had, and how his fleas had really made the scene. "

"THE SCENE?" the director cried. "NO WAY! YOU MADE THE PICTURE! YOU AND YOUR FLEAS SAVED MY MOVIE! I HAVE THE VISION NOW, I FINALLY KNOW WHAT THIS PICTURE IS ABOUT. THANK YOU!" He gave Opera a big kiss. "THANK YOU, THANK YOU, THANK YOU!"

The crew tried to raise the new hero to their shoulders. But it only took a couple attempts before they realized their backs weren't as young as they used to be.

And me? I kind of stood off to the side. No one even spoke to me. I couldn't believe it. Suddenly Opera was the hotshot. Suddenly Opera was the star. And the worst thing was I couldn't even hold it against him. After all, the guy was only trying to save my life.

Speaking of saving my life, I glanced over to Reptile Man. Gertrude's operator was pumping my teacher's hand up and down. It looked like he was pretty thankful, too.

Then, off in the distance I spotted Melissa Sue. She was stooping down to pick up Chad's toupee. She rose with it in her hands and clutched it to her chest. Even at that distance, I thought I could hear a faint, dreamy sigh.

Brock and his date were standing next to the little guy with the big megaphone. He was bragging about how he could get her a job and make her a star, and she was swallowing everything he said, hook, line, and sinker. Brock, on the other hand, was staring off, lost in thought. I figured he was thinking of trading her in for a different model, one with a brain.

And Wall Street? She was on her hands and knees scooping up fleas. "They're going to be a collector's item," she shouted to me. "They're gonna make me a bundle!"

Suddenly Dad's hand was on my shoulder. "Nice job, Son." I looked up to him. He continued. "For a minute you had me worried, but I guess it was all planned, right?"

I tried to smile.

"And Mr. Feinstein and Laura Lottalips . . . "
He motioned toward the two of them sitting side
by side on a distant bench. They were sipping
Perrier and talking and laughing like they were
old buddies. "That was real genius, the way you
worked that out. Real genius, Son."

Again I tried to smile.

"But these fleas," he said slapping his neck and
rubbing his shoulder, "you think they could have
used fake fleas instead of the real thing."

"Well, you know Hollywood," I grinned, doing
some head scratching and shoulder slapping of my
own. "They hate being fake; they love everything
to be real."

Chapter 10

Wrapping Up

After two showers and a hot bath, I was still covered in fleas. I called up the pet store, but they said there were no such thing as flea collars for humans. I tried to explain what had happened, but they figured I was a prank caller and hung up. After all, what I described couldn't possibly happen—not to "real" people.

Obviously they hadn't lived in my world. I thought of going down there and hanging around the store for an hour or so. Just long enough for a few disasters and calamities to strike. (With my luck that's all the time it would take). But I figured it wouldn't be fair to the pets. So I pulled ol' Betsy out instead. Let's see, when we last left James Brawn he was unconscious on the cave floor as Lizard Lips was closing in . . .

"How will we wake him, how will we escape?" Poppin Fresh cries.

Just then the Kool-Aid Pitcher crashes through the back wall. (I didn't know how he pulled that off, but since this is getting near the end of the story, I guess anything goes.) "Quick everybody!" he shouts. "Follow me!"

"But what about James?"

"Too late!" Lizzie hisses as she shoves her giant snout into the cave. Her body is too big to fit, but at least she can get her head and mouth in.

...And that, my dear reader, is her undoing.

One whiff of Lizzie's breath (hey, even Listerine can't work forever) and James begins coughing and gagging. The fumes are so strong they wake him. Immediately he leaps to his super agent feet and shouts. "Friends, we cannot run! Lizard Lips must be stopped here! She must be stopped now!"

"But how?" the crowd shouts.

"Yessssss," Lizzie laughs, as she flicks her forked tongue back and forth. "How?..."

"We must all work together!" he shouts

The crowd murmurs in protest.

"You must put aside your differences. You must stop treating one as more important than the other. We are brothers! Equally loved! Equally needed!"

"So what do we do?" someone shouts.

"Doublemint twins . . . take that gum you're chewing and stick it around Lizzie's neck to hold her in place.

Before the lizard can respond, the twins leap to action and accomplish their task.

Lizzie laughs, "I may be stuck, Brawn, but I can still see and hear, ...and I can still eat!"

"Keebler Elves!" he shouts. "Put some cookies over her eyes. Cap'n Crunch, Trix Rabbit run to her ears. Start crunching your cereal in them nice and loud so she can't hear."

Everyone obeys, but Lizzie doesn't seem worried. "An 'A' for effort Jamessssss, but you forgot my nosssse. I can sssstill find you and gobble you up with my sssssensee of sssssmell."

"Ronald! Colonel! Get in there with your chicken and burgers and confuse her with your wonderful aromas!"

They quickly obey.

"Toga Man!"

"Pizza, Pizza."

"Take that thick stringy cheese and wrap up her snout good and tight."

Toga man leaps to action and begins tying her mouth shut.

"Jamesss, sssstop thissss you mumm muop mmm...mmmm, mmmm, mmmm."

"Excellent!" James shouts. "Now Energizer Bunny, Duracell Dancers, toss me your batteries for this TV remote in my hand."

They do. And before you can say, "Is this getting weird or what?" he shoves the batteries in, points the remote control unit at Lizzie, and presses "Rewind." Just like that, ol' Lizard Lips shoots backwards out of the cave, across the sand, and into her own hole of a home...at about a zillion miles an hour.

The crowd cheers and raises James to their shoulders.

"No," James shouts, "not me. I'm only your average, run-of-the-mill, super-good-looking secret agent. You are the real heroes. You worked together....You

treated each other as equals. Now go
home, get back into those TVs and do us
proud."

Everyone shouts and claps as each one
of them heads back to Hollywierd. They
all are smarter, wiser, and perhaps a
bit closer to understanding how they
should treat each other.

James watches proudly. Yes, it's another
incredibly intelligent and indescribably
interesting job done by (Ta-da-daaaa!)
there's that good-guy music again...
Secret Agent Brawn, James Brawn.

I pressed F10, closed the computer, and smiled.
Not bad. I wished real life was that simple. There
were still a lot of things that needed fixing. You
know, the way I treated people, the way people
treated me. But I suppose that would all work out.
It would have to.

* * * * *

Three and a half months later, Opera and I
stood outside the Mall's Cineplex. "Mutant Monster from Mars" was playing. Every critic in the
world hated it. (Come to think about it, so did

every person in the world.) But that wasn't going
to stop Opera and me. No sir. We had our alle-
giance, we had our loyalty, and we had the twenty
bucks Dad gave us to see it.

"It's the least I can do," he said while dishing out
the dough. "After all, if it weren't for you boys, Mr.
Feinstein would never have given me that raise."

"If that's the case, how 'bout another ten for
food?" I asked.

Dad gave me one of his looks, and I gave him
one of my shrugs. What was it Pastor Bergman
always said, "You have not because you ask not"?

Now we stood outside the theater staring at the
poster. It featured Opera. That's right, my best
buddy was in the center of the poster, bigger than
life (if that's possible). He was held between
Gertrude's hissing jaws. And his mouth was open
wide in a scream for his life. The caption below read:

**They came, they saw,
they did as they pleased.
And worst of all, they carried...
FLEAS!**

"I'm sorry they cut you out of the film," Opera
apologized for about the hundredth time.

"Hey, don't worry about it. You're a better
screamer than I ever dreamed of being."

Opera nodded as he finished off another taco, "I guess it comes with all that classical voice training."

"I deserved it," I admitted. "Actually I deserved a lot worse than that, considering how mean I treated you and everything."

"We all learned a lot," Opera agreed as he washed down his last bite with an entire jumbo diet drink . . . all in one gulp.

And he was right, we had learned a lot. I mean besides the usual stuff—like, "Don't believe what you see in the movies," or "Superstars are just people like us (except for their hair pieces, extra makeup, and all the fakey stuff)"—we learned something else. . . .

We learned not to treat people different just because they have more money or popularity or whatever. God loves everybody, so everyone should be treated the same. In fact, if anything, people with less should be treated better than those who—

"Hey, Dork-oid!" It was one of the Metal Heads.

"Me?" I asked glancing around.

"Who do ya think I'm talkin' to, Salamander Breath? Now git outta da way so I ken see da poster."

"Oh . . . " I said, backing up. "Sorry."

Now where was I . . . oh, yes. That people with less should actually be treated better than—

"Ow! That's my toe, Slime Bucket!"

I twirled around, and accidentally stepped on his other foot . . .

"Get out of here, will ya?"

. . . Then I stumbled backward into someone else. . . .

"Look out! It's a Dork-oid!"

. . . and landed flat on my back staring straight up at Melissa Sue and her group of "Melissa Sue Wanna Be's." Of course, everyone had a good laugh. Only this time it wasn't *with* me, it was *at* me. I felt pretty crummy and wished I wasn't there. But that's okay, as far as Melissa Sue was concerned, I wasn't. I mean she looked right at me, but it was like she didn't see me.

I guess not everybody learned the lesson. I suppose some people like Melissa Sue and her group will just keep playing the Fame Game until they die. Too bad. As far as I can see, it's a game nobody wins.

"Step right up. Get your souvenir Flea Chains— get 'em right here."

I recognized the voice and scrambled to my feet. It was Wall Street. She had set up a little booth with a sign that read, "Going Out of Business Sale."

"Hey, Wally, wanna buy a Flea Chain?" she called.

"A *flea chain?*"

"That's right, a key chain with an authentic flea molded in clear plastic."

"How much?" I asked.

"A buck a piece."

"A buck a piece!" I shouted. "For a flea?"

"Not just *a* flea but one that starred in the movie."

I hesitated.

"Come on McDoogle, it'll be a collector's item. Tell you what, I'll make you a deal."

"What kinda deal?" I asked, already suspecting the worse.

"Since you're a friend and since I'm going out of business, instead of one Flea Chain for a dollar I'll give you two genuine Flea Chains for two-fifty."

I dug into my pocket. Good ol' Wall Street, some things never change. It's nice to know you can always rely on your friends.

ABOUT THE AUTHOR

Bill Myers is the author and co-creator of the best-selling "McGee and Me!" book and video series, which has sold 1.8 million episodes and has appeared several times as ABC's Weekend Special. He has written more than three dozen books and his work as a film maker has earned over 40 national and international awards. When he's not roaming the world making movies, he enjoys speaking at conferences and working with the youth of his local church. Bill lives in California with his wife, Brenda, and their two children.